For Herb Wright
and David Gerrold,
with love and thanks
for being there.

"YOU HAVE A WAY OF ASKING DIFFICULT QUESTIONS," SPOCK SAID . . .

T'Pris nodded, quietly acknowledging the fact. "So my parents said, and so said my husband. But now I am *T'Sai* T'Pris, *Aduna* Sepel *kiran*. For humans, a widow. For Vulcans, free to choose a new mate." She turned to look directly at him. "Or a lover. *That* is a difficult question to consider."

"I am betrothed," he said softly.

"But not wed," she said as softly. "Not yet."

Spock studied her for a long moment, considering what he knew of her, what he felt for her, the surprising emotions she called up in him. And he remembered what he knew of T'Pring, what he felt for *her*. The only emotions T'Pring brought forth in him were duty and obligation laid on him by others.

Slowly, he reached out his hand to T'Pris.

Lightly, gently, almost fearfully, their fingers touched and caressed.

STAR TREK

VULCAN'S GLORY

D. C. FONTANA

BASED UPON STAR TREK
CREATED BY
GENE RODDENBERRY

POCKET BOOKS
New York   London   Toronto   Sydney   Areta

POCKET BOOKS, a division of Simon & Schuster, Inc.
1230 Avenue of the Americas, New York, NY 10020

This book is a work of fiction. Names, characters, places, and incidents are products of the author's imagination or are used fictitiously. Any resemblance to actual events or locales or persons, living or dead, is entirely coincidental.

Copyright © 2006 CBS Studios Inc. All Rights Reserved.
STAR TREK and related marks are trademarks of CBS Studios Inc.

 CBS and the CBS EYE logo are
trademarks of CBS Broadcasting Inc.
All Rights Reserved.

This book is published by Pocket Books, a division of Simon & Schuster, Inc., under exclusive license from CBS Studios Inc.

Originally published in 1989 by Pocket Books

All rights reserved, including the right to reproduce this book or portions thereof in any form whatsoever. For information address Pocket Books, 1230 Avenue of the Americas, New York, NY 10020

ISBN-13: 978-1-4165-2462-5
ISBN-10:   1-4165-2462-2

This Pocket Books paperback edition August 2006

10 9 8 7 6 5 4 3 2 1

POCKET and colophon are registered trademarks of
Simon & Schuster, Inc.

Cover art by Cliff Nielsen

Manufactured in the United States of America

For information regarding special discounts for bulk purchases, please contact Simon & Schuster Special Sales at 1-800-456-6798 or business@simonandschuster.com.

VULCAN'S GLORY

Chapter One

THE SUNSET AT Ka'a Beach was glorious. Pink streamers and golden-bottomed cumulus clouds floated serenely above the orange glow that still tinged the distant dark horizon line of the sea. Thick tropical foliage in a range of vibrant green tones cloaked the flank of the steep mountain that rose behind the secluded beach, and several birds soared lazily on the gentle breeze off the ocean. The waves were soft, surprising for a late December day; and they crept in ever-extending laps farther and farther up the sand as the golden sunset slowly began to fade.

Spock ignored it all, sitting on the beach staring at his naked toes half-buried under the yellow-white sand. His boots, socks carefully folded inside, stood primly beside him. He had come to Ka'a for its quiet and its privacy, both of which had been zealously protected by Kauai's local government. The northernmost gem of Hawaii's necklace of islands maintained its right to preserve its natural beauty and had managed to do so for three centuries. Spock had been drawn to the Garden Island by its extreme contrast to his home planet.

He pulled his Starfleet jacket more closely around his shoulders as the wind off the sea rose slightly. He disliked cold weather of any kind; indeed, his personal quarters were always kept well above levels most humans appreciated. Vulcan would never experience such a cool wind as the one that now ruffled his hair. No lush vegetation ran such a riot of natural growth as on this tropical island, untended by nurturing hands. There were wide parklands around every Vulcan city and town, carefully maintained by squads of volunteer gardeners who felt a truly civilized society must spend some time among the tranquillity of growing things. But every tree, plant, vine, grass, and flower that grew in the parklands had been either botanically created by careful mutation and hybridization or imported from off-world sources.

Much of his planet was desert, relieved only by the ragged hulks of mountain ranges and the great blood-red oceans. Hardy succulents, gnarled and tiny-leaved *isuke* bushes, and *karanji*—similar to Earth's barrel cactus—constituted much of the wild flora of Vulcan. The flame-leaved *induku* trees clustered in the oases that had originally dotted the deserts—except, of course, on Vulcan's Forge. *Nothing* grew on the Forge, that immense blistering range of hellish sand and rock into which no one—not even the most toughened and experienced Vulcan—ventured willingly, or for long.

Spock reflected briefly on his own taste of the Forge,

images flickering in his mind of the ritual *kahs-wan* ordeal every Vulcan child underwent on his or her tenth birthday. It was a rite of passage, an endurance and survival test of the individual's strength, courage, and logic. (A tiny, ironic smile tugged at the corners of Spock's mouth. Intelligence was a foregone conclusion for a Vulcan child.)

There had been so many peculiar incidents tied up in his own *kahs-wan* that he sometimes thought of it as the single most important turning point in his life. He clearly remembered every event leading to and involved in his test, including the fact that he had set off for it unauthorized, alone, and ahead of schedule in order to prove himself a true Vulcan and not—*not* —an Earther.

He recalled his stubbornly determined march into the Forge, an impulsive act brought on by his father's stern admonition that he *must* learn to behave like a Vulcan. Spock had known Sarek was correct. Spock was subject to anger then, often fighting with Vulcan boys who taunted him about his half-human blood, and even giving way to tears of disappointment and frustration. It was a weakness that would not be tolerated in an heir by his noble clan. Spock had known he must conquer it, and forcing the *kahs-wan* had been his solution—even though doing so in such an impulsive way was another demonstration of his human heritage.

Fat old I-chaya, his pet *sehlat,* had lumbered after him into the Forge, refusing to turn back even after Spock had firmly ordered him to go home. And it had been a good thing the loyal old beast had followed him so relentlessly, because I-chaya had saved Spock from an attacking *le-matya*. The aging *sehlat* had charged and parried the *le-matya*'s attempt to get at the boy, until Spock's cousin miraculously appeared to finally subdue the great tigerlike beast with a skillfully applied neck pinch.

His cousin Selek had had an explanation for how he had discovered Spock had gone alone into the Forge and how he had followed the boy. It had seemed plausible at the time, and Spock had been desperate to get help for I-chaya, who had been wounded by the *le-matya*'s poisonous claws. There had been Spock's anxious hurry to reach and persuade a healer to come to I-chaya's aid, his grief over I-chaya's terrible suffering, and, finally, the decision required of him—to allow the healer to ease the *sehlat*'s agony by a painless and merciful death with dignity. Somehow, thinking back on it, Spock had never been quite certain of the logic of Selek's explanations. His parents' relief and pleasure over Spock's passing of the *kahs-wan* had diverted his attention from it, and Selek *had* shown him exactly how to execute the Vulcan neck pinch, a technique that had eluded Spock to that point. Still, he looked back every now and then and pondered the unusual set of coincidences that had provided him with such a perceptive cousin exactly when he needed him. Several years later, Spock had idly investigated the many branches of his family tree, but he could not seem to find exactly the right combination of "distant relatives" with those names who had a son named Selek. Somehow the information never seemed to be urgent enough for him to launch a thorough search, and in time he was far too busy to think about it. The most important thing the *kahs-wan* had accomplished was that it left Spock with the firm resolution that he would follow the Vulcan way, as his father and tradition demanded.

Spock sighed and shook his head. Denying his human heritage was a denial of his mother, and he could not dishonor her that way. Instead, he had gone on to strengthen those human qualities most like a Vulcan's and had learned to sublimate the more embarrassing ones. *Mostly learned to sublimate,* he reminded himself. He still remembered I-chaya proudly, but always with a swell of grief that put a lump in his throat.

Spock wiggled his toes. It had been an impulse to remove his boots and socks and sink his feet into the warm, fine sand. His mother had told him she had always enjoyed doing that. "Walking on a beach in your shoes is a joyless experience, Spock," she often said. "Put yourself in touch with the land . . . feel its *life.*"

A soft hiss and slap of water on the sand brought his head up. The tide had lifted a gentle froth of white foam nearly to his feet, leaving a dark, moist mark as it slid away again. Dusk was already pulling down the shadows, darkening the tropical growth behind him. Above the last faintly glowing light of the sun on the horizon, the stars had begun to appear, glittering with icy white and pale blue points. Spock freed his toes and brushed his feet free of sand. Quickly pulling on socks and boots, he managed to scramble out of the path of the next wave before he got damp. The temperature had dropped farther as the wind rose again. He pulled his jacket edges together and sealed them with a brush of his hand up the join. As he started to walk back toward the path through the undergrowth to the road, he realized he had not gotten all the sand off his feet. The grains shifted and bit into his flesh as he strode along toward the parking area where he had left his ground car. He ignored the discomfort but mildly cursed the impulse that had caused it.

The short-hopper whisked Spock from the Lihue shuttle field to Honolulu's spaceport. He carried only a light trip valise containing the few items he required for brief stays, plus two uniforms and a traditional Vulcan robe. Captain Daniels had ordered him to take some R&R after he signed off the *Artemis,* and he had gone with few possessions. Everything else would be forwarded automatically to his new ship.

"Spock, you work too hard," Daniels had said. "You're *not* always on duty. It's a commendable attitude for a young officer, but it's not practical." The captain had softened the remark with a smile. "Take the time to get away before you report to the *Enterprise.* Relax. Enjoy *not* having to tend to duty."

"I do require some time to review the *Enterprise's* expedition logs and equipment specifications," Spock had replied thoughtfully. "Especially the library computer and science station. I have not made a complete study of the ship's systems. . . ."

"That's not what I meant," Daniels snapped.

Spock had raised an eyebrow quizzically, the rest of his face perfectly composed. It was his best way of responding to anything that amazed, amused, or puzzled him. "Sir?"

Daniels stood up and leaned on his knuckles on the desktop. He put firmness in his voice and bit off every word clearly and sharply. "This is an order, Mr. Spock. You will go somewhere beautiful. You will take no research information with you in any form, nor will you access said information from Starfleet sources. You will relax. Swim. Walk. Ride. Lie on a beach if that's what you fancy. *But do not work.* Am I understood?"

"Yes, sir. I am ordered to relax."

"Excellent."

"Sir?" Daniels swiveled a wary look at him. "Captain Pike has a reputation as a taskmaster—"

Daniels interrupted sharply. "Chris Pike is hard but fair. Remember it."

"Of course, sir." Spock remembered everything. Automatically. Without effort. "However, I believe he will expect his new second officer to know something more about his vessel than its basic specifications."

"What are you getting at?"

"How many days am I ordered to relax, sir?"

"Ah." Daniels gave the question a few seconds' thought and then gravely replied, "You have two weeks. Ten days should be sufficient."

"Yes, sir. Ten days' relaxation. Is that all, sir?"

"Not quite." The captain held out his hand. "You've been an excellent third for me. I was happy to recommend your promotion, and I was even more happy to hear of your posting to the *Enterprise.* She's a fine ship commanded by an excellent captain. Good luck, Spock."

"Thank you, sir." Spock shook Daniels's hand quickly, exerting an acceptable amount of pressure. Then he dropped it, promptly clasping his hands behind his back, his usual stance when in the presence of senior officers. He had never been comfortable with the human custom of shaking hands. He much preferred the ancient ritual greeting used by Vulcans: "Live long and prosper." It was both formal and courteous and at the same time offered respect and good wishes. Spock considered it a prime example of Vulcan efficiency to convey so much in such a brief salutation.

The landing of the short-hopper at the spaceport interrupted his musings about the start of his leave. He collected his trip valise from the overhead storage bin and hurried out into the bustling port. He hadn't been scheduled to return here for another four days. Events had conspired to interrupt the ordered relaxation period the afternoon of his sixth day on Kauai. The subspace radio message had been relayed to him at the hostel via the *Artemis:* "Return to Vulcan immediately. Urgent matters require your attention." It was succinctly signed "Sarek." Daniels had attached a brief message of his own: "Sorry. I believe his orders supersede mine." Spock had sighed and gone to arrange for his return to the Honolulu spaceport, a connector shuttle to Armstrong Lunaport, and a reservation on a fast passenger ship to Vulcan.

Now, as he scanned a status board to confirm that his connector shuttle would leave on time, Spock wondered again what possible matters could be so urgent that only he personally could deal with them—

and which also required his presence on Vulcan instead of being transacted by subspace messages. It was remarkably convenient that the order from Sarek (and Daniels was correct; it most definitely was an *order* from Spock's father) should have arrived at exactly the time Spock was free to respond.

Of course, it would have taken very little effort on Sarek's part to discover that his son had received a promotion to full lieutenant and been transferred to the *Enterprise,* with an accompanying amount of leave time before being required to report. A Federation ambassador (even one not currently on diplomatic assignment) had more than enough Starfleet contacts to know every movement in his son's career. Not that Sarek personally would have sought out the information. He would have delegated the chore to an aide and would expect to find the data reported on his library computer with continuous updates. Sarek might never refer to it, but woe betide the unfortunate aide who failed to ensure that the most recent facts were there if wanted.

Yes, Spock decided, Sarek had known exactly where he was and that he could easily return to Vulcan for whatever "urgent matters" required him. Sarek would never interfere with Spock's duty by demanding that Spock take a personal-time leave. But he would not scruple for a second about interrupting Spock's official leave.

The connector shuttle was on time, and Spock turned toward the ticket counter where a reservations robot would confirm his place on board. Spock had hesitated briefly and then obeyed the summons from his father. Not to do so was unthinkable. Still, he wondered with just a twitch of uneasiness what it was all about. Sarek of Vulcan had not communicated with his son by written or spoken word for eight years—and they could have been light-years, so great was the philosophical distance between them.

The afternoon was getting on, and the hard yellow light of Vulcan's sun stretched long shadows across the courtyard, running in wavy ripples over the carefully raked ridges of the sand garden. As Amanda watched, the slim shadow finger cast by the candlestick tree touched the base of the highest rock in the group of three clustered together in the center of the garden. She could tell the hour almost to the exact moment as the dark line slowly lifted toward the rock's center.

Sarek would be home soon. And Spock—she sighed heavily—Spock would return to Vulcan in two days. She knew Sarek had planned it out very carefully, calculating all the parameters and possibilities. Two days was the maximum time it could possibly take for their son to receive the message, debate it, resist it, give in, and take transport to Vulcan. But come he would. Then there would be the confrontation between Sarek and Spock—not face to face, of course. Sarek had already arranged that, and Amanda had had to agree to his plan. Her title was *T'Sai* Amanda, *Aduna* Sarek—rendered inadequately but closely enough in English as the Lady Amanda, Life Partner of Sarek. She had accepted the role, but the choosing had always been Sarek's. She had wanted him more than anything else in any world that could be named, but it had to be *his* choice of her that made them life partners. Amanda had given everything she could to fulfill that role, and what Sarek had asked of her this time she would also do—but reluctantly.

She heard the outer door slide open exactly when she expected it. The candlestick tree shadow had touched the top of the highest rock in the sand garden. She turned toward the spacious foyer of the house, a smile automatically lifting her lips in spite of the sadness that rode her shoulders.

The tall figure of her husband moved against the brightness of the skylit foyer, a dark silhouette until he stepped into the large, cool main room. He wore plain, somber clothes as always, a deep forest green suit today, the only highlight the heavy gold ring on the index finger of his left hand—the clan ring worn by the ranking male family member.

Sarek saw her moving toward him, and his brown eyes lit with warmth. "Amanda."

His rich, vibrant voice stirred her as it always did, and her smile brightened her face. "You're on time."

"I would have notified you if I were to be delayed."

"I know. I'm teasing."

The light in his eyes grew warmer. "A human characteristic I have never been able to fathom, my wife."

"Perhaps not, my husband," Amanda said lightly. "But you do let me indulge in it."

"Analyzing it is a fascinating hobby." Sarek lifted her hand in his, sobering quickly. "I have received word that Spock is on his way. He has left the

Honolulu spaceport and will depart Armstrong Lunaport for Vulcan at five o'clock Earth time."

"Then he'll arrive in two days, just as you said."

"Of course."

Amanda turned away, pulling her hand from his. "Why are you forcing this now, Sarek? You know it doesn't have to be now."

"We have gone over the matter before, Amanda. Spock has obligations. It is his duty to fulfill them. The family, the bonds that are in place, the traditions he has sworn to uphold as a Vulcan—*all* demand he respond now in the accepted manner."

Sometimes Amanda hated the traditions, hated the narrow line of action they forced Vulcans to follow. But she had accepted them herself when she accepted Sarek's love and proposal of marriage, had accepted the Vulcan role of life partner, had birthed and raised a child whom she knew must also abide by the same traditions. She had made a promise to the man she loved and the house into which she married that she would do so. She kept her promises—her own human tradition—but that didn't mean it was easy. This was another one of the times when it wasn't going to be easy.

She turned back to her husband. "He has obligations to Starfleet, too, Sarek. Even you acknowledge that."

"What he must do here is acceptable within Starfleet. It has no relation to his duties."

"I think you are not seeing the two in relation to each other, Sarek," Amanda said firmly. "They are two different things, and I do not believe Spock can fulfill both duties simultaneously. We used to have an old Earth saying, 'Something has to give.' It is very possible that Spock will have to consider *not* meeting one obligation or the other."

"Then that will be his decision. I am certain he will choose the correct one."

"The correct one by whose lights?" Amanda asked. "Yours or his?"

Sarek stared at her, not answering for a moment. Then he turned and walked toward the corridor leading to the bedrooms. "I will be in meditation," he said quietly. "I assume supper will be at the usual hour?"

"Of course, my husband," she said formally. She watched him until he disappeared down the hall, then she turned away toward the formal sand garden again. She slid aside the door that led to the patio and stepped out.

Vulcan's twilight heat pushed at her, not uncomfortable now in the winter of its year. There were times in the summer when she could not even look out at the glare from the surface of the sand garden, but now it lay soft and pleasantly shadowed in the last light. She sat down on the stone edge of the patio, pulled off the light sandals she wore, and burrowed her bare toes into the warm sand.

There. In her mind, she went back through the years to the Carmel beach where they had honeymooned. Typically, he had brought work with him, and after breakfast the first morning he settled himself at a computer console to tend to it. She had kissed the tip of his ear, laughing, and gone down to the beach. She was on her knees at a tide pool, examining the microcosm of life assembled there, when she glanced up and saw him approaching along the beach. He was determinedly trudging along—wearing boots, of all things—stopping now and then, apparently to study the seaweed and kelp, the shells, and the stones tossed up on the tawny beach sand by the waves.

She realized suddenly that she was probably "a sight," as her mother would have put it—dirty feet, disheveled hair, no makeup. He had never seen her like that, even in bed. Because of his innate formality, she had taken care always to look as perfectly groomed as possible. Later, he told her he thought he had never seen her look so lovely—slim as a gazelle, dark hair tossed by the wind, and beautiful blue eyes that looked at him with open candor and honesty—and love.

She had chided him lightly, teasingly, about the boots. A beach like this was half wasted if one walked on it in boots. She never did persuade him to remove them and wriggle his toes in the sand. Vulcan dignity simply did not descend that far. She began to realize then that the traditions observed by Sarek—by all Vulcans—were not subject to human influence, even in so light a thing as informality in leisure time. Certainly the greater traditions that governed their lives were untouched by contact with humans.

Her son was bound, and tied, by those traditions. Sometimes, not often but sometimes, she felt guilty about Spock's half-human heritage. She knew it troubled him, gave him pain, caused him grief, all of which he buried behind a stoic Vulcan bearing. But would she have said no to Sarek's wish for a child? She shook her head and smiled ironically. Of course not. She had desired Spock's birth as much as Sarek had. She wiggled her toes again in the warm sand of the garden's edge and sighed. She had never persuaded Sarek to go barefoot. That would have been too human.

Chapter Two

THE CITY OF SHIKAHR glittered in the heat of midday as Spock's ground car approached. Behind it, the black, forbidding range of the Llangon Hills thrust upward and formed a perfect and dramatic backdrop for the sparkling city. The banding strip of parkland around it softened the transition from harsh and arid desert to the attractive geometric shapes of the city buildings. Architecture was very carefully controlled so that no new structure was in disharmony with any of the established buildings. The streets were designed wide, with grass or trees running down a center strip and on the verges. There were no slidewalks—Vulcans preferred to walk—and pavement frequently gave way to paths that wound under the carefully planted nonnative trees that offered shade.

Spock left the ground car near the eastern gate, closest to his parents' home, and entered the city. This area was entirely residential, and few of the buildings were more than one story in height. Most of the homes were enclosed within walls of one kind or another. As a child, he had liked most the home of a neighbor whose garden "walls" were carefully trimmed climbing rose brambles. In summer, the high hedge bloomed with luscious blossoms in a pastel combination of pink and white and pale silvery lavender. As he approached it, he noticed that the wall of his parents' garden had acquired a vinelike plant that grew over much of it. Here and there, a delicate trumpet-shaped blue flower peeked out of the dark green foliage that clung to the wall. He thought that would have been his mother's doing. His father favored the symmetry of the sand garden, beautiful but severe.

The gate was unlatched, and Spock let himself in. Dutifully he had sent ahead a message that he was coming as ordered and giving his arrival time. The gate made no sound, and he knew he hadn't, either, but the front door of the house instantly slid open, and his mother stepped out, smiling.

"Spock." She held out her hands to him.

"Mother." He strode to her quickly, dropping the valise. He took her hands in his, squeezing them tightly.

She freed a hand to touch his cheek, knowing it was a human gesture, knowing he would permit it only because it was she who did it. "Five years since I saw you at your graduation from the Academy. I've missed you, son."

"I know. You say so when you write."

She laughed lightly. "Of course I do." She studied him critically. "You look well."

"And you, Mother." She did look healthy and not

much changed from the way he remembered her. The softly clinging blue-gray gown she wore revealed that her figure was still slight, not gathering weight now that she was in her forties. He noticed a few more lines at the corners of her eyes and even several wisps of gray that had never been in her dark hair before. But the gentle beauty of her face was the same, as was the soft lilt of her voice.

A smile sparkled in her blue eyes. "And I see Starfleet has seen fit to promote you to full lieutenant. Ahead of time, I would guess."

Spock looked back at her solemnly. "I had anticipated my promotion would occur at this time. My service record and tours of duty have been sufficient to—"

"Spock, do you plan everything in your life now? When you were a child, you had spontaneity, you loved surprises—"

He clasped his hands behind his back, unconsciously echoing his father's move when he didn't wish to discuss a subject. "I am not a child."

"No." Amanda sighed as she looked at him. "Long ago and far away now. Well." She found another smile for him. "You're home for a few days, anyway."

"I am here because I was sent for, which you very well know. What is it he wants?"

"I can't discuss that with you here. After dinner, Sarek wants a family council. A formal council."

Spock's eyebrows arched in surprise—it was controlled, but surprise nonetheless. "Then he will speak with me."

Amanda shook her head. This was the part that was

going to be difficult to explain, and she didn't want to do it now, not when Spock had just arrived home. "Not exactly. Come inside now. You'll understand later."

Spock picked up the valise and allowed her to precede him into the cool reaches of the house. His father would not *exactly* speak to him? What exactly did Sarek intend to do?

Spock and Amanda ate alone. It was understandable that Sarek had chosen not to join them. The family council would probably not be a pleasant social affair. Trying to lead up to it with a family meal at which two of the participants hadn't conversed for eight years would be expecting far too much.

Amanda chatted quietly, asked questions, passing on any news that had occurred between her last letter to him and the present. She had always been someone who could tell a story, and Spock was amused by some of the incidents she described. Even the family news, incidents to be treated with some seriousness, was made interesting and diverting by her lively delivery of the facts. In return, he told her of his promotion and assignment to the U.S.S. *Enterprise* and of his brief relaxation trip.

"Ka'a? A lovely beach," she said, smiling at him. "Did you walk there?"

"In fact, I sat there. Thinking."

"A sea beach does have a conducive atmosphere for it."

Spock sipped at a glass of water, slid a sideways look at her. "I did remove my boots, however."

"Ah. Very good, Spock."

"It was instructive, as you always said."

Amanda tilted her head, her eyes sparkling with humor. "I never said it was 'instructive,' dear. I said it was something you do to feel in touch with the earth, with nature. You must *feel* it. It can't be taught."

"I . . ." Spock paused, cleared his throat, and started again. "I felt some of that."

Amanda reached over and lightly touched his hand. "I'm glad." The soft, mellow chime of the timepiece in the hall announced the hour. Amanda looked up, biting her lip slightly. "Time."

The room chosen for the council was the library, adjacent to Sarek's study. Bookshelves dominated three walls; the fourth wall contained a large window that looked out on the sand garden. The books on the shelves came from many worlds and covered a myriad of subjects, including nonfiction, poetry, and literature. Comfortable reading chairs were scattered around the room. Spock had spent hours here as a child, happily lost in worlds of information or imagination. This evening did not promise to be as happy or as satisfying.

Amanda settled herself in one of the chairs and gestured for him to take another. Spock shook his head and remained standing, waiting for Sarek. His mother picked up a tiny bead from a side table and placed it in her ear. "Sarek won't be here, Spock."

He swung around toward her, a frown suddenly creasing his forehead. "Then why has a family council been called? I do not understand."

"Your father will monitor from his study." Amanda indicated the small observer camera that would carry the image to Sarek's viewscreen. "And I will convey his words to you verbatim." She gestured apologetically toward the communication bead in her ear. "It is his wish."

So that was it. Sarek would have his say on whatever this matter was, but he would not speak directly to Spock. Their personal conflict from eight years before had not been resolved, and Sarek still refused to communicate with his son.

Spock had decided on a career in Starfleet and had applied to the Academy on his own, despite the fact that he had been just sixteen years old. His superior scholastic record had gotten him accepted instantly. He had been required to list his family background as a matter of course, and the superintendent of Starfleet Academy had routinely sent congratulations on his son's acceptance to Ambassador Sarek.

Unfortunately, Sarek had wished Spock to follow a career in sciences and research and had planned his son's attendance at the Vulcan Science Academy. The fact that Spock had not only decided on another course but had already engineered its beginning infuriated Sarek. Not that it showed; the anger was obvious only in the cold glitter in his eyes, the thin straight line of his mouth.

Amanda had insisted that they discuss it. The "discussion" had consisted of each of them taking a hard position and holding it, not giving an inch to the other. It had ended in Sarek turning away from his son, saying, "Do as you wish. We will not speak of this again." After a month of cold silence, Spock finally realized Sarek meant *he* would never speak to *Spock* again.

Spock nodded to Amanda and lifted his hands in an acquiescent gesture. "As my father desires."

"You may be seated."

"I would prefer to stand," Spock replied stiffly. "Please go ahead."

"Sarek wishes you to realize that you have been remiss in carrying out your obligations to your hereditary estate."

"I am afraid I do not understand such a statement from my father," Spock said bluntly. "The estate of Keldeen is managed in my absence by Senak of Zayus. He came to me well recommended by T'Lan of Lan, who manages my father's hereditary estate when *he* is off planet. Keldeen is not only producing a higher crop average than anticipated and making a profit, but new land has been cleared to include experimental crop planting. Therefore—"

"Unfortunately," Amanda broke in, "all this proves is that my son has chosen well in his estate manager." Her face was carefully controlled as she repeated her husband's words. "You point out this is the case with my—with Sarek's estate. True. But Sarek would point out to you that he periodically returns from his ambassadorial assignments to attend the estate himself. In eight years, you have not returned to Vulcan. You had to be summoned here at this time. Vulcan tradition requires that you personally attend to the affairs of your land as you are able. The fact that it has been managed well and made a profit is not in question. It is the matter of your involvement."

"Starfleet does not allow me that luxury. I have sworn an oath to carry out the duties I am assigned as an officer. I cannot violate that oath, and I will not resign. I can only swear to you that I will continue to retain an efficient estate manager, with whom I will remain in as close communication as possible. The benefits of our experimental crop research will naturally accrue to the family."

Amanda listened, nodded slowly. "You are still required to return as often as you are able to carry out this obligation yourself. That is, as often as your duty will allow. Sarek agrees you cannot break your oath to Starfleet."

Spock felt some of the tension leave him. If this were all, this enforced visit home might not be as uncomfortable as he had anticipated.

"However," Amanda went on, "the estate is not the only matter which requires your attention. There is something else." She paused, her eyes flickering uncertainly over Spock's face. "There is the matter of your betrothed. T'Pring."

Spock's expression did not change, but he felt a light jolt of apprehension at the mention of T'Pring. The maintenance and passage of hereditary land was an ancient tradition in many cultures. Spock could understand it and acknowledge its value in the heritage of a clan. But the betrothal of children with the obligation to marry upon maturity was something he found uncomfortable, even though it had been a Vulcan practice for thousands of generations. Was it only because he was obliged against his will? Or was it his human half, his rebellious half, that refused to accept as willingly as he accepted other traditions?

"What of T'Pring?"

"It is time to end your betrothal and plan your marriage."

"We barely know each other," Spock said. "We have not seen each other for years. She seldom even communicates with me."

"That does not negate your bonding. She is well chosen for you."

"Yes, by all standards she is. She is beautiful, she comes from a sufficiently high-ranking house, and she is full Vulcan. But did it never occur to you that I might have preferred to make my own choice, as you did when you married Mother?"

Amanda pushed to her feet, speaking for herself, not for Sarek. "Spock, that's unfair. Sarek was unbonded and free to choose."

"His parents broke tradition by not having him bonded to a Vulcan female in childhood. Sarek broke tradition by choosing you, a human woman. Why am I not allowed to break tradition as well?"

"You are the first and only child of Sarek, heir to this house. You may not."

Spock stood stiffly, staring at his mother, knowing Sarek watched coldly at his viewscreen. Something in him whispered that he did not want to obey, and something else held that whisper in check. Finally, he glanced toward the observer camera and nodded. "I understand. But it should also be understood that it is impossible for me to marry immediately. I am due to report aboard the *Enterprise* in a matter of days, and that order cannot be overridden. I do not know how long my first mission aboard her will take—perhaps years. The arrangements will have to be made for . . . the next time I return to Vulcan."

Amanda paused, listening, then smiled wistfully. "That will be acceptable. You will have to see T'Pring as soon as possible to discuss the arrangements."

"Tomorrow, then. Good night, Mother." Spock half bowed toward Amanda and left the room.

She stood a moment, fumbling the communication bead from her ear. Sarek appeared quietly beside her, waiting there silently until she turned to him.

"I realize that was not pleasant for you, my wife," he said quietly.

"I am not the one whose life is being dealt with here. I was lucky, I know. The traditions that bind Spock didn't bind you, and *we* were possible. We created him. Have you no feeling for the human side of him, Sarek? You chose me, and therefore you are also responsible for that facet of your son."

His dark eyes shadowed. Possibly there were doubts there, but Sarek would never admit them. "He has chosen the Vulcan way. For him, then, there is only the one path. His companion is T'Pring, chosen in the honorable Vulcan manner to be his wife and life partner."

"Whether he wants her or not?"

"How can he not want her? Spock admitted T'Pring is a beautiful Vulcan woman of a noble house."

Amanda shook her head, staring up at her tall husband. "If that's all that mattered, what am *I* doing here?"

For once, Sarek of Vulcan had no answer.

* * *

The U.S.S. *Enterprise* floated in Bay 14 of the San Francisco fleet spacedock like a spider caught in a web. Maintenance shuttles hovered around her, feeding the cluster of dockers on her hull with tools and power for the work being done on the big ship. She was only two years out of the launchways, but technology bounded ahead so rapidly that she would have been carrying outdated equipment if she weren't undergoing upgrade now.

Number One piloted the small one-person shuttle smoothly around and over the huge disk of the saucer, her eyes expertly and critically flicking over the work in progress. She mentally assessed and catalogued every operation, its status, automatically logging projected completion time. As soon as she completed her circuit of the entire ship, she rolled the little craft over and goosed it toward the closed shuttle-bay doors on the upper saucer hull.

"Number One to Shuttle Bay Chief," she snapped into the ship's communicator link.

The answer came back instantly. *"Shuttle bay."*

"Heads up. I'm coming home."

"Yes, ma'am."

The doors ahead of her slowly began to part. She cut in her braking thrusters, the gentlest touch, and the little shuttle slowed, allowing her enough time to slip through the opening doors with two inches to spare on port and starboard. She hovered the craft over the landing marker at center deck and eased it down. Because she had chosen not to wear a pressure suit while in the shuttle, she had to wait for the chief to close the outer doors and cycle the bay back to normal. She spent the time composing her report to the captain. The chief finally signaled the all clear. She clambered out of the shuttle, the report clear in her mind and ready for dictation into the computer.

She had no sooner stepped into the main corridor when the intership went on with the characteristic high warbling notes of the bosun's whistle. *"Number One, please report to Captain Pike in the briefing room."* The executive officer glanced at a chronometer and frowned. Her tour around the hull had taken longer than she planned; she was late for her meeting with the captain. She stepped to a nearby wall communicator and punched the button.

"This is Number One. On my way."

Captain Christopher Pike waited in the briefing room, knowing exactly how Number One would enter. He was not disappointed. The door slid aside for the exec, and the tall woman strode in briskly, information comp chips in her hand. "Reporting as ordered, sir. I'm sorry I'm late . . ."

"No apologies needed," Pike said amiably. "I would like to have gone on that outside tour of the ship myself. How's she coming along?"

"All the new equipment should be installed by eleven hundred tomorrow. We can set up a series of test runs to cover the next two days. No problem on meeting our departure date." She held out the comp chips. "I have the new personnel records ready for your examination."

"Let's see them, Number One."

Her long black hair swung forward over her shoulders as she sat at the table across from him, swiftly dropping a chip into the base of the viewscreen control console. Pike watched her, admiring again the high, slanting cheekbones and the startlingly deep blue eyes that made the woman's face so striking. She had a natural attraction that drew men's interest. He hid a smile, remembering two fleet officers who had blatantly followed her around Starbase 13, hoping to get a welcoming look from those eyes. No joy for them. Number One did not encourage advances. As far as Pike knew, she socialized with her fellow officers, but never on an intimate basis. In the four years she had served him as first officer, first on the old *Yorktown* and then on the new *Enterprise,* she had carried out her duties with a precision and perfection he had never seen in anyone else. In fact, *perfect* was exactly the adjective he applied to her at all times. He often felt he would like to know Number One better, to be closer to her in friendship; but her naturally correct, crisp attitude toward him threw up to him the same barriers he had seen her raise against the two officers on Starbase 13. Pike had resigned himself simply to having the best first officer in the fleet.

"Second Officer Lieutenant Spock, serial number S179-276SP. Reporting from the U.S.S. *Artemis.*"

"I'm not sure I'm going to like a Vulcan on the bridge, Number One." Pike shifted a little uncomfortably as the exec's eyes fastened on him. "I've never worked closely with one before." She continued to stare at him, waiting for him to go on.

When he didn't, she asked neutrally, "Do you foresee some difficulty, sir?"

"It's—well, they're logical to a fault. And maybe

that's the problem. I believe there are times when command personnel have to 'gut out' decisions, go on their best instincts. Cold, calculating efficiency isn't always the best reaction in a tight situation."

"Efficiency on the bridge has never troubled you before," she remarked dryly.

Pike winced inwardly. She was as cool and efficient as a Vulcan herself, and he knew he had never had a quarrel with any of her responses in any situation. "Besides," she went on, "Lieutenant Spock is only half-Vulcan." She tabbed the viewscreen control console, and the screen promptly displayed a personal background file on the young officer. "Father: Ambassador Sarek of Vulcan. Mother: the former Amanda Grayson of Colorado Springs, Colorado. Home base: the city of ShiKahr on Vulcan. Standard Vulcan education. Entered Starfleet Academy at the age of sixteen—interesting that he applied for entry himself. Qualified with the most outstanding grades of any cadet candidate of that class as well as the usual superlative Vulcan physical capabilities . . ."

"No 'weaknesses' because of his human heritage?" Pike's question was only half serious. Number One took it at face value.

"None revealed. His record at the Academy is brilliant, majoring in the sciences and computer technology. Graduation at the age of nineteen." Number One glanced at Pike and tapped the viewscreen. "He did the two years in the accelerated Vulcan course and one year in the required cadet working cruises aboard various ships. Once commissioned, he served for three years as assistant science officer on a space cutter in Sol system. Two years ago, he was promoted to lieutenant (j.g.) and has been serving as third officer and science officer on the *Artemis*—long-range cruises. On several occasions he has received commendations for heroic action in planetary exploration difficulties and has distinguished himself twice in scientific research. Despite deep-space service, he has continued to upgrade his computer specialist rating. He is currently an A-5."

Pike looked up in surprise. "The best rating most officers ever make is an A-3."

"Precisely, sir." Her dark blue eyes were amused as she stared at him. Pike dropped his own gaze, a little uncomfortable. "Yes, I see," he said quietly. He cleared his throat. "Personal ratings, relationships with officers and crew?"

"Generally good. His commanders' remarks are attached to the end of the service jacket, if you care to go over them. The lieutenant is reserved by nature but has no trouble working with crew or superior officers. Captain Daniels notes that Spock has also been known to play a Vulcan lute on occasion. Not a paragon, probably not perfect, either. He *is* half-human, after all." Number One smiled at Pike slightly. "But pretty damned good on the face of this record."

"*My* record looks good on the face of it, Number One. But I have to tell you there are some whopping mistakes recorded in it that I made when I was a young lieutenant."

"You survived them, sir."

"And I suppose we'll survive having a very young

Vulcan science officer as second on the *Enterprise*. Very well. Who's next?"

The exec punched up another record on the viewscreen. "Lieutenant (j.g.) Montgomery Scott, engineering officer, serial number SE-197-514 . . ."

Chapter Three

T'PRING LIVED ON her father's estate of In-Yar, which lay sixty kilometers outside the city perimeter. Spock's ground car had been speeding along a road that knifed through the estate grounds for ten kilometers. The final approach was lined with trees; the metal gates to the estate stood open. He was expected.

Spock drove through and parked beside a graceful fountain that spilled sparkling blue water into a free-form basin and then recycled it through the fountain system. Butter-yellow water flowers floated serenely on the surface of the basin, and a small darter fly flickered down to rest on one of the broad petals, ignoring the soft whisper as Spock cut the ground car's engine. Spock emerged slowly from the vehicle and paused to stare thoughtfully into the fountain for a moment, admiring the fragile beauty of the water flowers.

The house that rose behind him was two-storied,

constructed of dark stone quarried from the Llangon Hills. Its walls might have seemed forbidding, were they not softened by a drapery of climbing vines that sported bright red-orange blossoms. The second-story balconies were festooned with the flowers, and the vines reached even farther up the high walls, almost to the roof. Silvery curtains reflected the already intense morning sun back at the sky, shining in Spock's eyes as he looked at the house.

He didn't see the slight movement of one of the drapes in a second-story window as he walked toward the entrance door.

T'Pring turned away from the window as her father said, "It is he?"

"Yes, of course. On time."

Solen grunted. "If you can call six years late 'on time.' You should have been married at eighteen."

T'Pring shrugged as if this was of little importance. "He has been off-world since he was sixteen. We all know how the Academy and Starfleet service have demanded his attention since then."

"It seems to me, daughter, that you are remarkably patient in regard to your marriage. Your betrothal has gone on far beyond what any respectable clan would judge reasonable—"

"Because of my betrothed's commitments, which no respectable clan would, in honor, expect him to break," T'Pring interrupted coolly. It was a response Solen had heard from her many times when he raised the subject of her marriage. The sweet chime of the entry bell rang downstairs, and she gestured slightly to indicate it. "Now Spock is here to discuss the matter, it will be settled."

"I will greet him downstairs. Will you wish to see him in the garden?"

"It will be more private that way, Father. You will agree our discussion *should* be private?"

Solen snorted again, but if he disagreed with T'Pring, he chose not to voice it. T'Pring knew she was a special concern to her father, the only daughter in a family of five children, her mother dead for ten years. Solen had chosen not to remarry, and no tutor had been able to strongly influence the girl's behavior in her teenage years. She had proceeded through her adolescence solemnly, steering her own course, keeping her own counsel. When Solen raised the subject of her long overdue marriage, T'Pring either ignored it or overrode his comments with strong remarks of her own about Spock's obligations to Starfleet and the honor with which he must remain responsible to them. Solen finally had become resigned to the fact that T'Pring would deal with the problem of her marriage in her own way and that any opinions he had in regard to it would not be taken into account by his daughter.

A murmur of voices from downstairs indicated the door had been opened and Spock ushered in. "I will send him to you," Solen muttered, and he hurried downstairs.

He found Senak, his youngest son, engaging Spock with questions about Starfleet and the ships on which he had served. The boy admired Spock, and Solen knew he was considering applying to the Academy himself. *But,* Solen told himself, *Senak is the youngest of my sons and has more freedom.* The three older heirs were already married and had produced sons of their own, choosing to follow traditional careers on Vulcan which placed them in service to their house and to the planet. Senak could be spared to a profession that would see him traveling light-years from his home. Spock's involvement with Starfleet was of more concern. This was the first time he had returned to Vulcan since leaving for the Academy. Still, he was the only male heir of Sarek, and their house was a noble one. Spock was rumored to conduct himself in a manner "more Vulcan than most Vulcans" because of his human blood, and Solen believed he would prove to be a worthy husband to T'Pring. Eventually.

Spock pulled his attention away from the boy's eager questions and raised his right hand in the Vulcan greeting gesture. "Live long and prosper, Solen of In-Yar."

"Peace and long life, Spock. It is Lieutenant Spock now?"

"It is."

"You have done well in so short a time. You are a credit to your house."

"As I hope to be to yours," Spock replied.

"My daughter waits for you in the garden. If you will follow me, I will take you to her and then send refreshments." Solen held out his hand to indicate the rear of the large foyer which cut through the center of the house. A shady expanse could be seen outside the double doors there. Spock nodded, and Solen started to walk ahead of him.

"Father, may I not ask one more question?" Senak said quickly.

"Later perhaps. Lieutenant Spock has business with your sister now."

The boy subsided, carefully hiding any disappointment he felt. He half bowed to Spock and disappeared into a side room, leaving the two older men alone. Solen moved toward the rear foyer doors and pushed them open. "She will be by the pool. It is one of her favorite places at this time of day." Solen gestured across the garden, where a path of flat black stones wandered under the trees. Then he stepped back into the house and closed the doors, leaving Spock alone.

Spock followed the path, moving slowly. Part of his dawdling was explained by the fact that he truly admired the beautiful planning in the garden that allowed native growth to combine with hybrids and off-world plants in the same manner as in the city parklands. There was an abundance of flowers to add bright color to the softer greens, blues, and yellows of the trees and decorative shrubs. But the greater part of his hesitation was based on a reluctance to face the young woman to whom he was expected to commit the rest of his personal life. She was, and always had been, too much of a stranger to him.

He reached the pool, a quiet spot overhung with tall trees and carpeted with thick grasses that softened his step. T'Pring sat on an elegantly carved stone bench beside the water, her head turned away as she watched the light wind stir a patch of purple Earth irises. The last time he had seen her, she had been a thin, big-eyed adolescent, showing the promise of the great beauty to come but not yet realized. He paused to study her as she appeared now and had to admit she was exquisite. She was not much taller than she had been eight years ago, but maturity had given her figure womanliness. The dark, almond-shaped eyes still dominated her face, but they were supported by high cheekbones and a genuinely sensual mouth. Her long black hair was simply dressed in a braid through which a silver-blue ribbon was woven. The ribbon matched the color of the softly clinging gown she wore. She sensed his presence and turned toward him, rising as he moved around the side of the pool to her.

"Spock."

"Live long and prosper, T'Pring," Spock responded ritually.

"Yes. A long time since we have met." Not the ritual response.

Spock studied her carefully as she gestured for him to join her on the bench. He decided to remain standing. She arched an eyebrow as she looked back at him, but she seated herself, choosing to ignore what might have been a rejection.

The man she saw before her had changed almost as much as she had. He had grown taller; his chest and shoulders had filled out and broadened. He was no longer the stripling he had been, lanky as a reed, almost gawky. His thick black hair was neatly cut, sideburns trimmed in the triangle shape unique to Starfleet officers. She wondered briefly at the quiet solemnity in his eyes. She remembered him as more lively, more rebellious.

"My responsibilities to Starfleet have kept me away."

She nodded curtly. "As I have had to explain

frequently to my family and friends. I have grown tired of that answer, Spock. I was given to understand that home leave was possible, even in Starfleet."

"Technically, it is. However, we were not always fortunate to be close enough to Vulcan for me to arrange transit in the leave time I had."

"And now?"

Spock hesitated, decided honesty was best. "I was on Earth, taking leave there before reporting to my new ship. I was ordered back to Vulcan."

"So if Sarek had not ordered you here, we would not be having this meeting. Do you find me so ugly, so unattractive?"

"You are very beautiful. I have always thought so."

"Then there is some other reason why you avoid our marriage?"

"I have explained that my duties require me to be elsewhere."

T'Pring abruptly pushed herself to her feet to face Spock. "You also have a duty to me. We have been promised since we were both seven."

"T'Pring, I wish to please you, as I am bound to do, but my Starfleet obligations have precluded it time and again. And if I seem to hesitate personally, it is only because I do not feel I know you. Even when we were children, we were not close."

"The way to change that is to *become* close." She reached out to touch her fingers to his. "With time, we will know each other well."

He didn't move away from her, but he felt nothing as her hand lay against his. There was something cool in her eyes, something calculating that disturbed him. "Time is precisely the problem. I am due back on

Earth in just five days. I must report to my ship, and I have no doubt we will be assigned a mission almost immediately. I cannot say with any certainty when I will be able to return to Vulcan."

Her eyes seemed to turn darker, colder. "You have been committed to our marriage. Before you leave Vulcan, you will announce it. I have *done* with humiliation and with making excuses for you."

"I cannot name a date—"

"Then you will pay the bride price, and you will continue to pay it until we are married."

Dowries were not paid by a bride's family on Vulcan. It was the husband who was deemed to be fortunate to gain such a life partner. From the formal announcement of marriage, the husband-to-be paid a monthly sum to the bride's family until the wedding took place. The money was used to provide for the woman's needs until her husband officially took on his marital responsibilities, even if the woman herself was wealthy, or involved in a career of her own, or both. The bride price varied according to the husband's wealth. By every standard on Vulcan, Spock was personally wealthy, and the price extracted for T'Pring would be very high.

"You ask a great deal of me."

She stood away from him, anger carefully controlled but evident in her dark eyes. "I ask a great deal of *you?* I have responsibilities to my house—and to yours by right of betrothal. We should have been married years ago. Your own heir should be alive today. You have refused to return to Vulcan of your own volition. What am I to assume but that I and my clan are being insulted?"

"That was never meant—"

"Then what *is* meant?"

Spock turned away, hands clasped behind his back. "I tell you, I cannot give you a marriage date. My missions will interfere." He looked back at her. "I know I have an obligation to you—to be a good husband, to behave in the correct Vulcan tradition. But I also have obligations to Starfleet, and those obligations require me to be away for years at a time. It is unfair, I grant you. But I *chose* to accept the responsibilities Starfleet puts upon me."

"Do you reject me as life partner because I was chosen for you?"

"No. I only say to you that perhaps you would wish another. I cannot be what you seem to want."

"I do not wish another. We are betrothed, and we *will be* married." Her voice dropped away to a whisper. "When it is possible. I will defer to you regarding the day."

"Until *pon farr?*" he asked suddenly.

She looked up at him, gauging him, and finally nodded. "Until *pon farr,* then. But you will announce our marriage now, and you will pay the bride price."

"As you say."

A quiet voice spoke deferentially behind them. "Refreshments."

They turned to see Senak carrying a tray as he approached them. It was laden with a large platter of dainty sweetmeats and tartlets, a pitcher of cool fruit-water, and a pot of the hot Vulcan drink *saya,* similar to Earth's herbal tea. The delicate crystalline glasses and cups tinkled almost like bells as they clinked lightly together on the tray.

Spock glanced at T'Pring. He didn't want to stay any longer, but it would be an insult not to accept the offering. She seemed to view it in the same way, waving at her brother to come closer.

"Put the tray on the bench, Senak."

The boy hurried forward and carefully lowered the tray to the bench. He looked up at Spock, about to say something, but T'Pring curtly cut it off. "You may leave." He nodded to her stiffly and moved away. T'Pring gracefully settled her body into a sitting position on the grass beside the bench, motioning Spock to join her. "What will you have, *saya* or the fruit-water?"

"Anything. The *saya* will do."

Unperturbed now, she poured the hot drink into a cup and passed it to him. He chose one of the tartlets and bit into it, consuming it in two bites. T'Pring took her time, nibbling daintily at the sweetmeats. The silence between them extended as he sipped at the *saya,* trying to dispose of it as quickly as decently possible. T'Pring seemed not to notice, drinking her fruit-water and staring out over the quiet pond toward the stand of trees beyond. Her profile was lovely, and Spock reflected that if that were all he wanted, he would have had no complaint about arranging their wedding; but he had always had reservations about T'Pring.

Even when they were children, she had had a shrewd aloofness, a calculating coldness about her, especially when he and she had been together. He hadn't known exactly how to read it then. Now it lay at the back of his mind, troubling him, although he didn't know why. Vulcans *were* cool by nature, reserved, holding back, but this was different. Even his father at his most shrewd did not have this kind of manipulative coldness. Spock admitted to himself that he had not truly dealt with the problem of their marriage; he had simply put it off until he would have to consummate it. *Pon farr* would force the decision upon him, but at least he knew that was some indeterminate time in the future. Because of his half-human heritage, he had biologically escaped *pon farr,* the maddening lust urge that turned Vulcans back into the undisciplined savages they had been before logic and reason came to rule their lives. Most Vulcan males experienced it for the first time when they had achieved the age of twenty and in seven-year cycles after that. He had dreaded its onset, but so far it had not happened to him. Doctors at the Academy and on his mission ships had run him through routine physicals many times. Several had expressed the opinion that his human blood might spare him from *pon farr* completely. If it occurred, however, he would have no choice in the matter but to succumb to the biological demon that hid in every Vulcan male; he would have to consummate the marriage with T'Pring immediately.

He had drunk the *saya,* and now he carefully placed the cup back on the tray and rose to his feet. "I must go. There are details about the estate I must discuss with my manager. I leave for Earth tomorrow to report to my ship."

T'Pring looked up at him, her face set. "And you will announce the marriage."

"Yes. Of course. Tonight."

"Goodbye, then. When you choose to return—or

when you have to—I will be here." She turned her attention away from him, her fingers hovering over another sweetmeat on the tray.

"Live long and prosper, T'Pring."

She merely nodded and picked up the tiny sweet she had chosen. She waited until she heard the door of the house close behind him before she got to her feet. Listening closely, she finally detected the soft purr of the ground car as it started and went out the gates. Then she moved quickly around the pool and into the stand of trees opposite the bench.

"Stonn."

The man who stepped toward her was all Vulcan, not as tall as Spock but brawny and darkly handsome. He held out his hand to her, and her fingers caressed his. "Will he announce the marriage?"

"Yes, it is done. He agreed to pay the bride price. He did not even ask how much it might be. And, Stonn, he agreed to let the marriage wait until his *pon farr.*"

"But that might be—"

"Never. I know. But I will still be his life-partner-to-be. The announcement will be recognized by all Vulcan, and he will pay and *continue* to pay because he is honorable." She playfully ran an index finger up the line of Stonn's jaw and then followed the shape of his outer ear up to the point, tickling him. "In the meantime, we have each other."

Stonn frowned at another thought. "If he does undergo *pon farr,* you will have to marry him."

T'Pring laughed softly, although her mouth barely smiled. "Even so, he has his precious Starfleet, and he will never stay here very long. When he is gone, we will still have each other." He started to say something, and she placed two fingers over his lips, following it with a light kiss. "And if he ever does decide to retire here, we will *still* have each other."

Stonn pulled her more closely to him. Her body was warm; her lips were soft as they roamed his neck.

Stonn wondered why he sometimes felt a chill quiver through him when he was with her.

Chapter Four

THE *ENTERPRISE* LOOKED MAGNIFICENT.

Spock studied the ship closely as he was ferried toward it on a transfer shuttle from the San Francisco spaceport. He could have beamed up via transporter with a good deal less trouble and time taken, but he had wanted to see his new ship from outside. While looks could be, and frequently were, deceiving, the *Enterprise* he saw in the huge spacedock was a taut, well-run ship—lean, powerful, eager for space. She had just been worked on, upgraded; everything about her was shining and in its place. She was lined up in the bay, ready to cast off the tethers that kept her leashed to the spacedock and nose out to where she could engage her impulse engines and *go*.

Several other officers and crew personnel had elected to take this shuttle with Spock, and most of them also had their eyes turned out the ports to study the ship that would be their home for a number of years to come. One young lieutenant moved around the transport craft as it began to angle up toward the giant saucer and the shuttle docking bay. The dark-haired officer seemed more interested in the engine nacelles than in the whole of the ship. A brilliant smile played around the man's face as he studied the exterior of the great pods. As he turned back to find his seat again, Spock caught a glimpse of the insignia on his uniform. *Of course,* Spock thought. *What else but an engineer?*

Pike was alerted to the arrival of the transfer shuttle carrying the last of the new crew members. As soon as they disembarked, they were met outside the shuttle bay by Number One, crisply greeting each by name and rank. She swiftly assigned them to their individual quarters and concluded with the information that the captain would speak to them all in the briefing room at thirteen hundred sharp. Then she left them to sort themselves out and find their way to their new homes.

Spock found his quarters easily; he had scanned the *Enterprise*'s blueprints on the voyage from Vulcan, committing them permanently to memory. He was not surprised at the size of the two-room accommodations, but the obvious comfort caused him to raise an appreciative eyebrow. The fleet's ship architects had apparently given much thought to the many possible Federation aliens who might occupy the space. There was a temperature control which could be set to suit a Vulcan's high requirement for heat; but it could also drop down far enough to accommodate a Tellarite, one of the bearish creatures who normally had to wear cold suits to tolerate the human temperatures that governed most ships. Spock was pleased to note the thermostat was already set high enough for his comfort. He had felt perpetually cold on the previous vessels on which he had served.

The lighting could also be adjusted to varying shades of brightness, according to the needs of the cabin's occupant. The furniture was Starfleet standard, but there were interesting little nooks and shelves and bare wall spaces where personal treasures could be hung or displayed. Spock's trunk had arrived and been left in the sleeping area. Glancing at a chronometer built into the spacious desk, he decided he had time to unpack and get his things stowed before he had to report to the briefing room. He bent himself to the chore.

Lieutenant (j.g.) Montgomery Scott had no trouble finding his quarters, either. He not only knew the blueprints of the ship intimately, but he had built an exact cutaway scale replica of the *Enterprise* as soon as he learned of his assignment to her. Her corridors and decks and service tunnels were already as familiar to him as his mother's house in Linlithgow, West Lothian, Scotland.

As an assistant engineering officer, and a junior one at that, he had been assigned a large two-room suite with another assistant engineer. Because of a carefully planned schedule of duty rotation, neither man would be on shift at the same time; and at the moment, his new roommate was on duty. He had left a message for Scott blinking on the viewscreen on the desk.

"Hello, Scott. I'm on engine-room duty, but make

yourself at home. If you have time, come by engineering and introduce yourself. Otherwise, I'll see you at 1600. Bob Brien."

Scott immediately started to unpack his baggage. The uniforms and off-duty clothes protected two of his most precious possessions. He lifted the top layer of uniform shirts and trousers from the chest and hung them in the small closet assigned to him. Then he pushed aside the long length of red Scott tartan that covered it and brought out the ancient fighting targe and its accompanying sheathed two-handed broadsword. They had been passed down in his family for centuries, eldest son to eldest son, and he would no more dream of going into space without them than he would dream of relying on engines he hadn't checked out personally. He looked around and found a suitable bulkhead wall between his bed and a stack of built-in shelves that would nicely accommodate the targe and sword. He dug out several metal-adhering hooks that would bear the weight of his two prizes and swiftly attached them to the wall. Then he lifted the old bronze-studded leather targe and the great sword into place and stood back to study their placement. *Yes*, he thought. *They belong there. I'm home.* Satisfied with his work, he turned back to the chest and started to bring out his engineering manuals.

The briefing room was moderately crowded with new personnel, both officers and crew, when the door slid open and Pike stepped through. Young Engineer Scott had chosen a place toward the front of the room, among a group of other engineering technicians.

Spock stood at the back of the group and studied the captain. With his superior height, he could see the man clearly, and he had to admit he was impressive. Captain Christopher Pike was approximately an inch shorter than Spock himself. He was an inordinately attractive man, graced with black hair, intensely blue eyes that seemed to notice everything, and a slim, well-muscled body. His voice was confident and friendly when he spoke.

"Welcome to the U.S.S. *Enterprise*. I am Captain Pike. I don't know you all individually yet, but I guarantee you I will before very long. That's not a threat." There was an appreciative chuckle from the people assembled. Pike flashed a brilliant smile at them, seeming to favor everyone. "The *Enterprise* is a small community, a family, if you will. I make it my business to know who everyone is. There may be times when my life and that of others will depend on what you do. I know there will be times when all of your lives will depend on what *I* do. I want to have complete confidence in you, as I hope you will have confidence in me. I believe Starfleet has always attracted the best and the brightest. I trust that you will prove my belief is sound. Our first mission together will be one that might be considered tame by most of you, something fairly routine. However..." And here Pike paused dramatically. "I can assure you that no mission is ever *just* routine. Every time we go out, we learn something. We blaze new trails into the unknown. But remember, space is not our ally. The *Enterprise* is. This is a fine ship, and I insist on a superior crew. I know you'll live up to my expectations." Pike glanced around and flashed his attractive smile again. "I look forward to meeting you all personally. Dismissed."

As the group began to break up, Pike's eyes moved over them critically and landed on Spock. "Mr. Spock."

Spock promptly stiffened to attention. "Yes, sir."

"Join me in my cabin, please. We have a few things to discuss."

"Very well, sir."

Spock followed the captain out of the briefing room, down a corridor, and into a turbolift. Pike didn't speak, and Spock felt he should not, either, under the circumstances. As the doors slid closed on them, Pike snapped, "Deck 5." The lift promptly began to glide downward.

"Have you met Number One, Mr. Spock?"

"Only in passing, sir. The executive officer greeted us upon arrival this afternoon."

"I'll expect you to work closely with her."

"Yes, sir."

"You have no problems with that?"

"No, sir. My record will show I have had good relations with all the first officers under whom I have served."

"Some officers have had a difficult time dealing with the fact that she is a genetically perfect being. On her planet, Ilyria, excellence is the only criterion that is accepted. She is technically designated as being the best of her breed for the year she was born."

"I see. She therefore would receive the appellation 'Number One' even if she were not the executive officer."

"You have it."

Spock thought it over briefly and flashed a sidelong glance at Pike as the turbolift slowed. "Vulcans do not indulge in genetic manipulation as such, sir. However, we have been known to do a great deal of selective mating to achieve the highest form of individual of which our society is capable. I believe I can understand Number One's background, and I have no difficulty in accepting it. I appreciate excellence in all its forms."

Pike glanced at him, wondering if Spock were making a joke. He decided he was not.

The turbolift had reached the uppermost quarters deck, and the doors snapped open. Spock's own quarters lay down the corridor to the left. Pike turned right, and Spock followed him along the curving corridor to the farthest door. Pike keyed his admission code into the pad on the wall, and the door obediently slid open. The suite inside was exactly the same size as Spock's, a fact he noted and approved. He was well aware the official captain's quarters on the *Enterprise* consisted of a three-room suite. Pike obviously had rejected it in favor of this smaller area, placing himself no better than his other senior officers.

The main room was plainly but comfortably furnished, all softly muted pastels. Spock noted approvingly the large cache of books on the shelves. From where he stood, he could read a number of the titles. Fiction and poetry mingled with nonfiction, technical manuals, and fleet regulations. Pike settled himself in an armchair and gestured Spock to a seat opposite him. "We push off in twenty-four hours, Mr. Spock. You'll be relieving Lieutenant Commander Davies at the science station and as second officer. When do you think you'll report ready?"

"If the commander would like to leave, sir, I could relieve him now."

Pike leaned forward, his blue eyes glittering with interest. "You haven't even toured the ship yet, Spock. Do you really think you're ready to take over?"

"Sir, I have studied every piece of information on the *Enterprise* that exists in Starfleet's open records. En route from Vulcan to Earth, I also accessed and reviewed the logs of all her missions to date. And, of course, I am well acquainted with the science station since that has been my area of expertise since Academy graduation."

"With honors," Pike said dryly.

"Yes, sir."

"And you undoubtedly studied the personnel list of the science officers who will be serving under you."

"Not the service jackets, of course. They are not files open for inspection from outside. However, I planned to do that as soon as this interview is over. I have looked over the ship's reports of current personnel performance which are a matter of log reports in the science section."

Pike leaned back in his chair. "So there *is* something you don't know, after all, Mr. Spock."

"Sir?"

"You'll have another new science officer on board, reporting in from service on the U.S.S. *Musashi*. An astrobiologist—and a Vulcan. Lieutenant T'Pris."

Spock's eyebrows lifted, then he quickly pulled his expression back to its usual solemnity. "I will examine her records with interest, sir. I am sure I will find the lieutenant has served with distinction to date and that she plans to continue to do so."

"Do I detect just a little prejudice toward Vulcans here?" Pike's eyes were smiling as he asked the question.

Spock's dark eyes met the captain's, and a hint of humor hovered there as he replied. "No more so than toward humans, sir. There are qualities in both races which I admire."

Lieutenant Bob Brien was a tall, lean man, almost six feet four, with a head of dark curly hair. Mischievous blue eyes twinkled beneath dark brows, and a cheerful smile frequently turned up the corners of his mouth. He returned to quarters promptly at sixteen hundred and found Scott unpacking the last of his possessions and neatly stowing them away.

"Montgomery Scott? Bob Brien." He held out his hand to the other engineer, and the two men shook. "Welcome aboard."

"Thanks. Sorry I dinna get down to engineering. There was the captain's welcoming, and then I found I have the graveyard shift tonight. I thought I'd best spend the time getting unpacked and set up here before I report on duty. I did do a review of the ship's engine maintenance schedule and current status . . ."

"You'll be fine. Chief Engineer Barry is a top hand, and she'll be there to brief you. Say, what do they call you? Monty?"

"Scotty." He shrugged and laid on his accent just a little more than usual. "It's a natural, I suppose."

Brien laughed in acknowledgment. "Scotty, then. I have a little welcoming for you myself." He turned to his side of the suite, rummaged in a drawer, and came out with an odd-shaped bottle of clear liquid.

"Well, I do appreciate a wee drop now and then," Scott said. He studied the bottle curiously. "No label."

"Nope." Brien set out two glasses and took the bottle from Scott.

"Is it what I think it is, then?"

"The best engine-room hooch you've ever tasted."

"Ah." Scott grinned at his new roommate. "Now, there's a subject on which I am an expert." Heavy drinking of any kind was frowned upon by Starfleet, of course. But long tradition had established the existence of engine-room hooch, and no one minded very much if bottles of the stuff were made and consumed for special occasions. Scott himself had headed up an undergraduate band of engineers at the Academy which had built and operated a busy little still in the generator room of the Administration Building that the superintendent had never discovered. Or, at least, the superintendent never admitted he had discovered it. It had been rumored the super liked a drop of the product himself now and then. Scott's primary concern was always his duty and his engines, but he never refused an opportunity to turn his hand to a little spirit making if time allowed and it didn't interfere with his responsibilities.

Scott took the proffered glass with its splash of clear liquid and upended it, downing the shot in one swallow. As the taste hit home, he nearly choked. "What the devil have you done to it?" he spluttered, gasping for air.

"What d'you mean? This is good stuff."

"If you like drinkin' bog water. Good grief, man, have you never had any *fine* liquor?"

Brien seemed offended. "Well, I admit it's the first bottle, but this is supposed to be the best in the fleet. We got the recipe from the *Lionheart,* and everybody knows *their* reputation for it is top of the line."

Scott snorted and set the glass down as if it were contaminated. "Everybody *knows* you don't give away your formula. And it's clear to me *Lionheart* didn't." He sighed. "Well, I can see there's work to be done on this. But just to get us off on the right foot, let me offer you something better."

He went to his closet and lifted down a precious bottle of Glenlivet. "Now, *this* will give you a taste of the better." He poured a splash into two fresh glasses and held one out to Brien.

The other man sipped and smiled appreciatively. "Of course, that's real whiskey."

"Laddie, when *I* turn my hand to engine-room hooch, you won't be able to tell the difference."

Brien's grin widened. He reached out and touched his glass to Scott's. "Welcome aboard the *Enterprise,* Scotty."

Spock's inspection of the science section was brisk and efficient. Lieutenant Commander Davies was happy to be relieved almost a full day ahead of time and only mildly surprised to discover that Spock required the most minimum of briefings to be brought up to date on the section. Davies left the Vulcan to the examination of personnel service jackets and hurried to his quarters to prepare to leave ship.

The service records of the crew members and

officers under him generally pleased Spock, though he expected no less than quality from anyone assigned to the *Enterprise*. He had just scanned Lieutenant T'Pris's records when the door of the science office swished open behind him. There was a soft-voiced "Pardon me, sir" behind him, and he turned to see the Vulcan woman standing serenely at the entrance.

"Lieutenant T'Pris. I am Lieutenant Spock."

She nodded slightly. "Yes, sir. I have the duty watch this shift."

Spock gestured her forward. "Please come in. There is very little for you to do except routine monitoring while we are in spacedock. I assume you will have some research projects in work once we are embarked."

She moved toward him gracefully, with the gentle glide of the classically trained Vulcan woman. She must have received instruction in the ancient ways when she was a child. Some families still believed in such traditions. Spock wondered whether or not she had felt the clash between the old arts and the far more technological and scientific teachings of the Academy. Her records indicated little of her personal background, but Spock recognized her house name as an ancient one, quite as old as his. Her family had an honorable heritage, first as military leaders when Vulcans embraced a more savage civilization, and then as advocates and counselors when Vulcan philosophy turned to logic and peace.

T'Pris had excellent academic achievement marks, as expected, and a commendable four-year service record. Spock also noted she was a widow of just over a year. Her husband, Lieutenant Sepel, had been killed in a violent alien encounter on Lindoria while both were serving on the *Musashi*. There were no specifics in regard to her husband's death in T'Pris's records. He recalled a few vague references to the incident, but none of the details. The few facts about it that had reached the *Artemis* had only mentioned the ambush of the landing party from the *Musashi*. In any event, it would have been discourteous of Spock to mention her bereavement. Such mention would have to come from her.

Spock could not help noticing that the woman herself was striking—taller than most Vulcan women, less well endowed in figure than T'Pring but slender and upright as a young willow. She had a classic Vulcan beauty, pitch-black hair wound in braids like a crown about her head and eyes of deep brown. Spock glanced away from her, suddenly aware of the subtle and clean scent of a Vulcan herbal soap she must favor in her bath.

"I completed all my research projects of the moment on the *Musashi*. I am sure new ones will present themselves on this ship." She held out her hand to him. "I am pleased to be serving with you, Spock of the house of Surak and the noble clan Talek-sendeen."

He touched her hand, gently pressing his right index finger against her slim one to acknowledge the ritual greeting. He was startled by the sudden electric feeling that shot through him, and he had to make an effort to steady his voice as he replied, "And I am pleased to be serving with you, T'Pris of the house of Sidak and the noble clan Ansa-sen-tar."

She did not seem to have been affected by the

touching of their hands as he had. "I hope I am not indiscreet in acknowledging family, Mr. Spock," she said gravely.

"Acknowledging family is our tradition," Spock responded quietly. He realized he was still touching her hand and pulled his away. "There are so few Vulcans in the fleet that the traditions are welcome."

The gentle smile that touched her face was beautiful. "If there are so few of us, then we must view each one as precious. Is that not so, Mr. Spock?"

Spock paused, thinking it over, mulling the consequences of what he would reply. Finally, he nodded. "Yes, Lieutenant. I would say that is so."

Chapter Five

THE BRIDGE WAS a busy place at any time, but especially so when the *Enterprise* was maneuvering for space. In addition to the usual duty complement, the chief medical officer, Dr. Philip Boyce, had also secured a place to watch the main viewscreen as Pike crisply gave the orders that nosed the great ship out of the spacedock. The curve of the Earth below glittered bright blue under scattered cloud cover, and the doctor sighed softly as it slipped out of sight.

Boyce had enjoyed his stay at home during the time the *Enterprise* had been in spacedock undergoing equipment upgrades and taking on new personnel. Odd how he always regarded his ramshackle bungalow on Cape Cod as home, despite the fact that he only got to occupy it for a month or so out of every several years. Alicia had passed away so early in their marriage that it seemed he had always been a bachelor. He had never cared to marry again after her death, but he had escorted his share of attractive ladies in his many tours of duty. He never brought any of them home to the Cape. He spent endless hours fishing when he was there, sometimes surf casting and sometimes from a small dinghy he liked to putt around in. He had felt there was little sense in planting a garden which was impossible for him to maintain and which would suffer from the blasting sea winds that roared across the Cape, especially in winter, but he enjoyed growing things. As a result, his personal quarters on ships always sported in place of pride several shallow tubs of earth, arrangements of small stones and carefully cultured and clipped grass, and graceful *bonsai* trees. He favored oak, birch, and maple.

Idly, he wondered if Chris Pike had had a satisfactory shore leave. The captain had been anxious to return home himself when they had docked, but Boyce had noticed a reluctance to discuss his trip when he came aboard to resume command of the *Enterprise. Well, Chris'll bring it up if he wants to talk about it,* Boyce thought. He had served with Pike for four years now and felt he knew him about as well as most senior officers knew each other. Often, Pike would use him as a sounding board on personal matters, things that were eating at him. And things did get to the captain, despite the cool, in-control persona he normally projected for the benefit of the crew. Doubt seldom seemed to intrude on Pike; but personal relationships, an awareness that sometimes he had to ignore his humanity in order to command, these bothered him.

Nothing seemed to be troubling him at this moment, however. Pike sat straight-backed in the command chair, alert to the tone and rhythms of the bridge instruments as the *Enterprise* finally cleared the dock. The sensors were busy, scanning far ahead, searching for clear space. Pike's voice quietly gave the maneuvering orders to Number One operating the helm console.

"Impulse power, Number One."

"Impulse power, aye."

Her long, slim fingers played swiftly over the panel, and the *Enterprise* began to pick up speed.

"Plot course to transit Sol system to jumpoff point."

"Course plotted, sir," Lieutenant Andela replied promptly from the navigation console beside Number One.

The ship leaped ahead, swiftly beginning the traverse of the system. Pike sat back in his chair and glanced over at the tall, lean, hawk-faced doctor. "Well, Phil, on our way again."

"Areta." Boyce shrugged. "We've made the trip before."

Pike grinned and shook his head. "You old space hound. You never even set foot on the planet."

"And whose fault is that? *You* were the one who got to go down and have a look 'round planetside. That doesn't obviate the fact that most of us went along with you on the trip to and from Areta."

Pike turned in his chair to look at Spock, busy at his science station. "Mr. Spock, for those on board who did not make the earlier trip to Areta, would you care to brief them on our destination?"

"Yes, sir." Spock moved his fingers over several control areas on his library-computer console, and the image of Areta flashed up on the main viewscreen and all other screens keyed to it. Spock's quiet, clipped voice was enhanced by the ship's intercom system as he concisely outlined the salient facts about the planet.

"Beta Circinus III, called Areta by its natives, is a Class M planet. One thousand four hundred fifty-seven years ago, warring factions unleashed a nuclear holocaust that devastated large areas of its surface. The planet has begun to regenerate itself but still has a vast expanse of what are called hotlands, radioactive wastes that are completely uninhabitable. The native populace itself is divided into three types, descendants of the original inhabitants, all of whom have survived on their own terms: townspeople, wandering tribes of nomads, and mutants. The mutants are the outcasts of the planet and are reported to be dangerous in the extreme. At this time, all three native classes are isolated from and highly hostile to each other. However, a few trade contacts between townspeople and nomads were established four years ago, largely through the efforts of Captain Pike. It is Starfleet's feeling that this civilization can again become viable and achieve harmony and growth if interaction between the functioning societies on the planet can be achieved, especially through trade."

"Thank you, Mr. Spock," Pike said. "That is our mission to the planet—to extend and enhance acceptance of mutual cooperation and trade between at least the nomads and the townspeople. My previous efforts were accompanied by a good deal of luck, which I'm hoping will hold through my next visit."

"That's what I said," Boyce snorted. "You're the only one who gets to go planetside."

The chief of security was not happy about the prospect of the captain beaming down alone to a planet surface. Lieutenant Commander Orloff had his four section commanders in his office, trying to come up with other alternatives they could present to the captain. Orloff was a short man, just squeaking past Starfleet height requirements, but taut and physically fit as a man a decade younger than his own thirty-eight years. The three lieutenants and one lieutenant (j.g.) who watched him stalking back and forth privately thought Orloff was taking this a little too seriously.

"Sir," Lieutenant Myoki Takahara pointed out, "the captain *has* beamed down to Areta alone once before."

"And he admits it was sheer luck that he linked up with a nomad tribe that were inclined to be friendly," Orloff shot back.

The dark-eyed officer glanced across at Daniel Reed and arched her eyebrow, the equivalent of a shrug for her. Reed frowned slightly, acknowledging the still pacing Orloff with a brief jerk of his head. "He did take precautions, sir."

"Certainly. He had survey team studies of native costume, charts of nomad movements, a recording of language analyzed and translated. Do you know how sketchy that information is when you're on the ground, mister? When you're on your own and flipping out a communicator just might get you killed, let alone what seeing that piece of technology could do to mess up the native civilization?"

Lieutenant (j.g.) Endel was a Kelyan, a reptilian humanoid with grayish scaly skin, a long, sinuous body, and a face incapable of a smile. Still, something about his bright, beady eyes suggested humor as he studied his superior officer. "Commander, none of our suggestions has been useful to you. Perhaps you have some plan of your own in mind to persuade the captain that he should not make this second appearance on Areta alone."

"He must be made to understand that captains do not make lone excursions to hostile planet surfaces," Orloff said obstinately.

"Perhaps other captains don't—and that's what you're used to," Lieutenant Pete Bryce said quietly. He glanced around at the others, his look reminding them that Orloff was new to the ship and new to Pike. Maybe Orloff didn't understand the nature of their captain, although Pike was certainly well enough known by reputation in the fleet. Pike led his people from the front, waving them on to keep up with him. Pike's view, often communicated to his officers, was that no commander was any good "leading" from the rear. "The view's bad, and the firsthand information isn't reliable" was his personal observation.

Takahara smiled pleasantly at her superior officer. "No matter what you have been used to, Captain Pike does not follow a common path."

"I've noticed," Orloff said snappishly.

"However, the captain *does* take suggestions," Endel pointed out.

"Meaning?"

"If you approached him with an alternative suggestion—not a demand, mind you, but a *suggestion*—he might be disposed to give it every consideration."

"The security chief has an obligation to protect the captain's person from any possible harm—"

Reed interrupted mildly but tellingly. "That is absolutely true, sir, but the captain is also the commander of this ship and has higher orders to follow. You can suggest ways that those orders might be more—*safely*—carried out. He'll listen. Whether he'll do it your way in the end or not . . . " Reed shrugged.

Orloff studied his junior officers thoughtfully. All of them had more time in service with Pike than he had. In that regard, they were far more experienced than he. "I think this might be a matter the captain and I should explore together."

Heads nodded around the table. Orloff felt he finally had a consensus of opinion on the best way to deal with the problem of the captain. It never occurred to him that the captain might consider *him* a problem.

Pike started out mildly amused at Orloff's concern, but his amusement degenerated rapidly into irritation when the security officer pursued the subject. The captain patiently listened to the man's presentation of his case, then waved his hand to cut the flow of talk when Orloff began to repeat himself. "Thank you, Commander. Your concern for my safety is appreciated, but I don't believe you've fully examined all the facts. The nomad tribes of Areta are extremely suspicious of strangers. A group of unknowns attempting to make contact with them would make the situation far more dangerous than one lone traveler, which is how I successfully presented myself."

"But, sir, to go down alone a second time—"

The piping call of the intercom sounded from Pike's desk, and Lieutenant Zacharia's soft, melodious voice spoke into the room. *"Communications to Captain Pike."*

Pike crossed to the comm and tabbed it. "Pike here."

"Sir, a message is coming in for you from Starfleet. Classified and priority."

"Route it to my screen, Lieutenant." He barely heard Zacharia's murmured assent as he turned to Orloff.

"I'll leave, sir," the security officer said immediately.

He rose to go, but Pike's voice arrested him in midmotion. "Mr. Orloff, I do know that you're only considering my safety, but I believe you should also consider the fact that I've served my time in the fleet, commanding three other vessels before this one. I've had a good many solo missions planetside." He held out his hands slightly, offering evidence. "Not a scratch, although I admit to some close calls."

"Close doesn't count. Death or serious injury does, sir," Orloff said brusquely.

Pike's eyes hardened into blue ice chips. "The point is taken, Mr. Orloff. I expect you to do your duty, but don't try to prevent me from doing mine."

Orloff opened his mouth to reply, thought better of it, and opted to sketch a half-salute and a murmured

"Yes, sir" to Pike. The captain glanced toward the door, and Orloff took the hint, almost leaping across the cabin to it. The door slid open just as he arrived before it, and Orloff quickly stepped through. It swished back into closed position behind him, and Pike was alone.

The intercom on the desk had begun to chime softly, a repeating signal of four notes that told Pike the confidential message had arrived and was waiting for him to receive it. When he leaned over to key it, the scrambled version first flashed up on the screen. Then the lettering wobbled and cleared into readable text. Pike read it through and keyed his intercom.

"Pike to Bridge. Mr. Spock."

"Spock here, sir."

"Please report to the briefing room immediately."

"Aye, sir."

The intercom went silent, and Pike smiled briefly. Spock continued to make a good impression. No questions or hesitations on the order, just a simple acknowledgment that he would obey instantly. Perhaps Number One had been correct. Pike had always appreciated having officers with intelligence and efficiency on his bridge.

Number One had glanced up from the command chair when Spock was paged by Pike. She, too, had been satisfied with Spock's response, and she noted that Spock promptly keyed the intercom to call in Lieutenant T'Pris to take over the science station in his absence. She counted off the seconds to herself and was pleased that it only took two minutes for the young Vulcan woman to appear on the bridge to relieve Spock. Everything correct, everything precise between the two. Number One personally preferred to run the bridge that way, though Pike liked a warmer, teamlike atmosphere when he was in the chair. It was all a matter of preference. When they arrived at Areta and Pike went down to the surface on a solo mission, she would be in temporary command, and the *Enterprise* crew would perform to her standards. Because the crew and the ship's readiness were her prime business as first officer, it pleased her to realize that no matter who she called on to perform, the ship and the crew would respond swiftly and precisely.

Spock reached the briefing room only minutes after Pike. The captain had had the time to insert a chip recording of the confidential message into the control console of the viewer at the end of the table. As Spock came into the room, Pike waved him to a seat. The Vulcan had barely begun to fold himself into a chair before Pike snapped, "What do you know about the Vulcan's Glory?"

"The same as every other Vulcan knows, Captain."

"Recap for me, please." Pike smiled suddenly. "I'm sure your knowledge of its history is far more complete than mine."

"I would say that is most likely, sir," Spock said equably. He paused a moment before he spoke, swiftly marshaling the facts as he knew them. "The Glory is an emerald of immense size—twenty-two thousand eight hundred ninety point four carats—clear deep green in color, uncut but reputedly almost flawless."

"That much is recorded." Pike nodded.

Spock looked inward and summoned the history as he spoke. "The stone was won as a prize of war in the year 1433 Vulcan calendar, extremely ancient by Terran reckoning. You may appreciate its age by the fact that Vulcans have not embraced a warlike philosophy for more than three thousand years. However, at the time it was won from the house of Kawarda, in the battle of Deen T'zal, it was so great a trophy of war that it was given the name by which we now know it, Vulcan's Glory."

"Why was the gem never cut?"

"It was the heart of the house of Kawarda. They felt the spirit of their clan dwelt in the stone. To own it was to own the soul—the very being—of the Kawarda. To cut it would have been unthinkable. It became a symbol of Vulcan and was placed in the stewardship of the clan Archenida, whose war leader Sorrd had actually captured the stone in battle."

"For centuries, the Archenida protected the Glory. Periodically, it was taken from Vulcan, always in the guardianship of the clan, and paraded in high ceremony among the exploration and merchant ships Vulcan sent out from the planet. In human terms, it might be called showing the flag. It was on such a ceremonial voyage that the ship *He-shii* carrying the Glory apparently suffered a fatal accident and vanished forever. Of course, the Glory vanished with it."

"According to the records, no debris was ever found at *He-shii*'s last known coordinates."

Surprisingly, Spock felt a twinge of sympathy pulling at him, a heaviness in his chest for the lost ship, its crew, and its treasure. He controlled it ruthlessly, pushing it down and away from his consciousness. "That is correct, Captain. It was concluded that the ship plunged out of control into unknown space, dead, or dying. For centuries, Vulcan engineers and astronomers have plotted every possible variation of the course she might have taken as unknown space became more and more explored and mapped. To date, no trace has ever been found of the *He-shii.*" He paused and then added quietly, "It was a great loss for Vulcan."

"The ship and its crew."

"And the Glory."

Pike studied Spock carefully, trying to gauge something he did not understand. "If the Glory was a prize of war, and Vulcan rejected the philosophy—the *emotion*—of war, why is the stone such a great loss?"

"In the time that it was captured, Vulcan warriors felt the spirit of the Glory had passed into them, that it had become the heart of all Vulcan, as it had been the heart of the Kawarda. When Vulcan's philosophy changed, the spirit of the Glory also changed, from war to peace, from passion to logic."

Spock wondered how he could explain to Pike the depth of meaning the Glory had for Vulcans. It was a symbol of the changes in the Vulcan soul and thought that made them the creatures they were now, the change that created the sophisticated civilization with its high moral, philosophical, and logical standards that governed Vulcans today.

Pike sighed and nodded. "As the highest-ranking Vulcan command officer aboard, Mr. Spock, you are entitled to know that the priority message I received contains some possible new information on the Glory."

Spock's dark eyes leveled on Pike's. "New information?"

Pike tabbed the control console, and a flood of figures flashed up on the screen. "A new extrapolation for the course of the *He-shii* has been put forth by Vulcan Science Academy theorists."

"T'Clar and Spens, no doubt."

Pike quirked an eyebrow in sardonic amusement. "Is it true Vulcans know everything?"

"No, sir. However, we do retain in memory everything we have ever learned."

"Thank you for that information, Mr. Spock. You're correct. Doctors Spens and T'Clar sent a robot probe along one of the projected courses the ship—if damaged and out of control—might have taken. After a long voyage, the probe revealed a small planet in its path. The planet's been tagged temporarily as GS391. The probe was not equipped to detect life forms."

"After so long, life would not be expected to sustain."

"No. But the probe did scan the planet's surface. There were indications of metallic debris. We have been ordered by Starfleet to divert to GS391 to investigate. I want you to head up the landing party."

Spock was silent a long moment, then he stirred. "I believe an all-Vulcan team would be appropriate, Captain."

"Very appropriate, Mr. Spock. Very appropriate indeed."

Number One twisted in midair and angled her body so she caromed off the side wall of the null-G ball court using her right leg to push her back toward the center. Chief Engineer Caitlin Barry had anticipated the move and shot in front of the exec, body-bloc her away from the ball. The collision of bodies sent them careening off in opposite directions, but Caitlin had managed to backhand the ball, slapping it toward the catch-trap goal in Number One's end of the court. As Number One somersaulted in the air to land with her feet against the end wall under Caitlin's goal, she saw the ball hurtle straight through the catch trap and in. The scoreboard honked and racked up the three points for the chief engineer.

"Lucky!" Number One shouted, but she was grinning.

"They all count!" Caitlin laughed back.

The two women pushed off the walls and shot back to their respective goals. Number One grabbed one of the soft holding straps on the wall and waited for the catch trap to drop the ball down to the launcher and snap it into play again.

Off-duty time during a routine mission often bored Number One. She grew restless when her shifts on the bridge were monotonously the same, and these one-on-one null-G ball games with the chief engineer helped work off the nagging frustration of her uneventful duty hours. Physically, she had no need of tension release; her musculature and stamina required only a minimum of rest to remain at peak performance level for long periods of time. It was her curious, probing mind that needed the action. Number One liked to lose herself in the strategy and physicality that null-G ball demanded so she could relieve the boredom of too many hours of simple routine. It was an odd "failing" her perfectionist genetic creators had overlooked.

She and Lieutenant Commander Barry were of an

age and had been in the same class at the Academy, though they had not been friends then. The demands of their separate courses of study—command and engineering—had drawn them into relationships with people with the same primary interests. Since being assigned to the *Enterprise,* however, the two women had found common grounds for a friendship. Caitlin was almost as tall as Number One, an auburn-haired, hazel-eyed woman whose beauty was not one whit diminished by the enchanting splash of freckles on her nose. She was not what many officers thought of as a typical engineer. She had high standards and demanded that meticulous care be taken with the equipment in her charge, but she was not in love with her engines. She was on top of all new engineering advances, but she did not spend all her spare time with technical manuals. She enjoyed her duty on the *Enterprise,* but she was not enthralled with the starship except as a masterfully designed craft. Many engineers lived and breathed their arcane craft; Caitlin had other interests that occupied her attention off duty. One of them was trying to beat the socks off Number One in one-on-one null-G ball. She was on her way to accomplishing that at the moment. She was ahead twenty-four to eighteen, with less than a minute left in the game.

"Let's see you make that shot again," Number One taunted.

"Let's see you make it at all," Caitlin heckled in return.

The ball dropped into the launcher. There was a moment's pause—the launcher was programmed to release on an irregular time sequence—and then the ball was rocketed into the court. Both women waited for its bounce off the far wall to judge its spin and direction, then they pushed off after it. It was headed almost directly at Caitlin, but Number One kicked straight up and intercepted it as it went overhead. She twisted to angle off the ceiling and slammed the ball sidearm toward Caitlin's goal.

It hit the outside edge of the catch trap and bounded away to the left. Caitlin snagged it as it passed her and gave a kick that pushed her toward Number One.

The executive officer arrowed at her, aiming a little low, and grabbed Caitlin's foot as they passed. The yank put Caitlin into a spin. She still had the ball but couldn't control her body at center court to take a shot.

Before she could get straightened out enough to get in a shot, Number One had bounced off the far wall and was on her way back. She reached out to slap the ball away, and it spun free of Caitlin's hands, hitting the floor and then heading up at an angle. Number One realized it was pure luck that her trajectory and the ball's coincided, but she willingly took the break it gave her. She grabbed the ball, managed to aim, and two-handed a shot at the goal. It sailed straight in, and the scoreboard obediently flashed up her three points —twenty-four to twenty-one. Then the game-ending horn hooted raucously. The gravity controller eased on, allowing the two women to lower themselves gently to the floor.

"Next time," Number One said mock-threateningly.

"I was just toying with you," Caitlin said cheerfully,

reaching for the towel she had left outside the court. *"Next* time, I'll really mop the deck with you."

The exec grinned at her. "Buy you a drink in the rec room."

"Good loser."

"No. You just don't win that often." She ducked the towel snap Caitlin aimed at her and trotted ahead of the engineer into the dressing room.

They climbed out of their shorts and workout shirts, showered, pulled on clean uniforms, and headed for the recreation room without much conversation. The place was only moderately full before dinner, but a few card players heckled one another over poker hands, and several vid fans had gathered around a viewer to watch one of the vidramas the ship had stocked for the voyage. Number One gestured to a food slot on the wall, and Caitlin said, "Herb tea is fine."

"Sounds good. I'll join you."

Number One tapped in the order, waited, and the two cups of aromatic brew were delivered piping hot in mugs a moment later.

Caitlin had settled at one of the smaller tables, and Number One joined her. They clinked mugs and sat back companionably, sipping at the tea.

"How's the department?" Number One asked.

Caitlin glanced at her, raising an eyebrow. "I give you a written report every day."

"And I read them. I wasn't asking for the formal language, Cait. How do you *feel* it's running?"

Caitlin considered, then nodded. "Good. Not great yet, but good." She caught Number One's questioning look and raised a hand to cut off the idea. "Oh, I don't mean there's anything wrong. The warp engines are tuned so fine there isn't a fraction of variance between them and the control specs. Starboard impulse engine's running a shade off, but nothing serious. I'll call for a recalibration when we get to Areta, just to be on the safe side, though."

"Personnel?"

"Veteran team is top notch. The new ones are settling in. The best of the group is that Scottish j.g."

"Scott."

Caitlin nodded. "Appropriately. Montgomery Scott. Engineering's in his blood and his brains. He does the right things on instinct while others have to stop and puzzle over it. He'll go a long way, I think. In fact, if I don't stay on my toes, I might find him promoted to chief over me."

"Not likely, Cait," Number One said, smiling.

"Well, not for a while. But he *is* good."

They sat silently for a moment, sipping at the tea. Then Caitlin nudged Number One. "How's the captain?"

"As in what?"

"As in, I usually get a full rundown from you on how he looks, how he seems to be feeling, what he's been doing. This time, no mention at all. Something wrong up there?" She lifted her eyes toward the ceiling to indicate the bridge.

The exec shook her head, studying the depths of her tea as if to read leaves in the bottom of the mug. "I don't know. Last time we based on Earth for R&R, he came back happy. He talked about this woman he met. I gathered it was serious."

"I remember your saying so."

"She's an Academy cadet now, but I was sure Chris"—she corrected quickly—"the captain would come back from this leave announcing the engagement. But . . . nothing. Not a word."

"Maybe he didn't get to see her. She could have been on one of the mandatory cadet cruises."

"Mmm."

"What were you hoping for?"

"Nothing."

"Number One, remember me? This is Caitlin you're talking to, not some stranger."

The exec silently studied her tea, and Caitlin studied her. Finally, Number One looked up at her friend. "I was hoping for an answer. He's engaged, he's married, something definite—not dead silence. He's been very preoccupied, even a little moody. It's not like him."

"Why does that bother you?"

"A happy captain means a happy ship."

"That's a cliché, and I don't believe you mean it. How long have you served with him now, four years?" Number One nodded. Caitlin considered it, then she said quietly, "You know, I never asked you how important Chris Pike is to you."

"He's my commanding officer."

"I had the impression he means more to you than that."

"Caitlin . . ."

"Now I'm sure of it."

"Cait."

"Maybe something happened between him and this woman. Maybe it's time you let him know how you feel about him."

"I can't do that. I—I don't feel anything toward him."

Caitlin snorted in aggravation. "You might be genetically supreme by your planet's standards, Number One, but you're a rotten liar. What you mean is, you don't want to let him know how you feel. I understand. You work closely with him. And it's not just on the bridge. You've backed him when he's been in dangerous situations planetside. You're both professionals, and you think the relationship could be compromised if it gets personal. On the other hand, there are married couples in command posts on other ships. The relationship could be *strengthened*. Did you ever think of that?"

"He doesn't—couldn't—" Number One stammered, then blurted, "He thinks I'm perfect!"

"I know a lot of women who'd give anything to have a man like Chris Pike think that about them."

"Perfect for them and perfect as applied to me are two different things."

Caitlin studied her friend for a long moment, knowing she sometimes felt odd and out of place, despite her poise and strength of personality. Genetic engineering was common on several planets, but it was normally used to correct potential birth defects and other errors of nature. Number One, however, had been completely "designed and engineered," with an emphasis on intelligence, even temperament, strength, and a pleasing appearance. She was the product of someone else's idea of what a perfect woman should be. As it happened, a good many people agreed with the design engineer, but . . .

"I think you're projecting your view of yourself

onto him. Why don't you find out what *he* thinks? Let him know how you feel."

"I . . . might."

"Yes."

"If he's free."

"Yes."

"If it's off duty."

"Yes."

"And if I have the nerve."

The so-called graveyard shift was entirely satisfactory for Lieutenant (j.g.) Montgomery Scott's extracurricular activity. The ship kept a day and night schedule, and during the graveyard shift most work areas were nightlit to assist the nocturnal illusion. There was never less than a full complement on duty in the engine room, but the chief engineer and assistant chief seldom stood that watch themselves. Engine-room personnel, therefore, were fairly free to amuse themselves as they wished.

The hardware Scott had concocted in the past few days was intricate but not terribly large. Since the members of his shift knew what he was up to and were sworn to secrecy, he could construct his invention without fear of revelation. Bob Brien appeared in the engine room at 0200, his mischievous blue eyes twinkling in anticipation. "Do you have it, Scotty?"

"Of course, man. Do you like the look of it?" Scott moved to a console and lifted the tubing-and-container contraption into view from behind it. It was spindly and awkward and not entirely beautiful.

"We-e-ell . . ."

"Och, man, you've no eye for the engineering of it,"

Scott said disparagingly. "Look here." He pointed out its salient features. "The ingredients go in *here*, the boiler." His finger traced along the slim silver line of piping from the bulbous lump to the next streamlined square of metal. "Through the coil to the collector, where it all comes together and . . ." He paused reverently. ". . . *Meshes.*" Scott moved his hand along the final line of piping as he finished. "And out through the pipe into any receptacle capable of holding one-hundred-percent *true* engine-room hooch."

"It seems so simple," Brien said doubtfully. "We had something like this when we followed the *Lionheart*'s recipe."

Scott snorted disdainfully. "This is just the *mechanism*, man. The recipe, now, that's a secret known only to the practitioners of the art. And if you think the *Lionheart* crew would give it to you, you'd believe in many a thing that doesn't exist in this world or any other. *My* recipe, now, is a fact. It came from the lowlands, from the soft and smoky hills, and it has *age* on it, *history* on it. A thousand years of Scotts brewin' it. It's bewitched and bedeviled and an enchanter besides. And on top of that"—Scott grinned broadly —"it's a mighty good drink."

Brien smiled back. "I believe it, Scotty. But where do you plan to put that thing? We can't leave it here in the engine room."

"No? Try this." Scott carried the contraption over to the tangle of pipes that drew coolant off the core where dilithium crystals underwent the bombardment that transformed matter and antimatter into usable power for the warp engines. He shifted the peculiar piece into a position that seemed to meld right into the pipe puzzle. "I can link it in here. Stand off a pace, and you can't tell there's anything strange about it being there. Look closer, and it seems like an extra piece of piping in the system. It just draws a bit of heat off the core for the boiling process—no harm done to anyone—but the result is one sweet batch of engine-room hooch."

"You're sure?"

"Sure as sure can be."

Chapter Six

GS391, AN UNPREPOSSESSING PLANET when the ship's sensors first touched it on orbital approach, proved to be equally unappetizing close up. Spock read out the gloomy statistics from the science station as they flashed up on the screen above his console. T'Pris stood beside him, logging a copy of the readout into her tricorder for use on the surface when the landing party beamed down.

"Smaller than Earth, only marginally a Class M planet. No bodies of water that qualify as oceans, but there are thirteen large lakes that may be considered inland seas. Six major land masses characterized uniformly with low mountains, plains areas studded with grasses and small trees, best described as a veldt. No higher-intelligence life forms. Birds and insects predominate, but there are some small carnivores and herbivores, nothing on the mammal intelligence scale as high as apes or dolphins. It is an old planet, wearing away, uncultivated and unpopulated."

"No signs of habitation at all, Mr. Spock?"

"None detected, Captain. However, the robot probe was correct in reporting large pieces of shaped metal. They are located in the southwestern hemisphere, scattered over approximately two square miles of terrain."

"Can you determine the nature of the debris with ship's sensors?" This from Number One.

Spock leaned over his console, his long, thin fingers swiftly tapping controls that defined and refined the information being received by the long-range eyes of the ship. Finally, he glanced up, significantly looking at T'Pris before he looked at Pike. "Sensor analysis of its alloy content indicates the metal debris is ancient Vulcan in its origin."

"The *He-shii*," T'Pris murmured.

"The odds are astronomically in favor of it," Spock agreed.

Pike swung around in his chair and nodded to the two Vulcan officers. "Get your landing party down there and verify, Mr. Spock."

Spock was already heading for the lift door, T'Pris close on his heels. "Aye, sir. We'll beam down in nine minutes and six seconds." The lift doors swished open at their approach, and Spock half turned to lock eyes with Pike. The captain was staring at him in some amusement at the preciseness of the time specification. "My people have been standing by in the transporter room, waiting for your order to go."

"Thank you for that enlightenment," Pike said wryly. "I'll expect a report from you in ten minutes and ten seconds. Or thereabouts."

The small team of Vulcans that waited for Spock

and T'Pris in Transporter Room 2 was a mixed group of specialists—an engineer, an astrophysicist, a computer analyst/technician, and a junior navigator. There were eleven other Vulcans on board, but Spock had chosen a representative cross-section of age and clan to comprise the landing party.

They turned toward him and T'Pris as if drawn by a string as they stepped into the transporter room. "There is no doubt in my mind that the unnatural metallic objects on the planet surface are the remains of a spaceship," Spock announced. "If it proves to be the wreck of the *He-shii,* it may be possible Vulcan will finally regain the Glory."

"May it be so," the astrophysicist, Sefor, intoned.

The others echoed it ritually. "May it be so."

Spock nodded, and they took their places on the transporter platform. The transporter chief waited until they were all correctly positioned, then said, "Ready, sir. I have locked coordinates onto the middle of the debris field."

"Energize."

The shimmering glow of the transporter grew over the six figures, covering them. As the mechanical hum rose to its peak, the glow abruptly vanished, taking the Vulcans with it.

They rematerialized on an undulating plain carpeted with thick wild grass that stirred slightly in a low breeze. As they looked around in silence, T'Pris automatically turned on her tricorder and scanned the nearby debris.

The shattered pieces of metal that lay strewn across the landscape bore witness to catastrophe. The ship had died violently. The searing heat of an unbraked entry into the atmosphere left burn scars deep in the metal. Clearly, she had been ruptured and broken as she came down in her blazing death throes. Parts of her uniquely shaped hull had fallen in a pattern consistent with explosions that hurled wreckage from high above, not from impact with the ground. The transporter chief had put them down close to the largest piece of hull section. It was the last and barest bone of a ship—weather, age, and small predators had worn and nibbled it down to the outer skin.

"The metal is definitely of Vulcan origin." T'Pris's voice was low and controlled. She hesitated in what might have been a trace of emotion just once. "From the degree of . . . of deterioration from exposure to weather and natural erosion, its age is approximately—"

"It is the *He-shii,*" Spock interrupted flatly. He pointed to the faint trace of lettering that trailed up the side of the large hull piece. The ancient Vulcan script was barely readable as the last part of the ship's name and a portion of its identification number.

The odds of recovering anything intact from this desolate wreck were so low that Spock did not bother to waste time calculating them. Still, he moved toward the large piece of barren hull, more in curiosity than in the hope of finding anything. T'Pris dutifully followed him, scanning. Their tricorders might be able to detect and analyze clues, something—anything—that might hint at what had happened to the *He-shii.*

As Spock and T'Pris stepped within three meters of the hulk, a metallic, grating voice suddenly spoke. It took a second for Spock to recognize the words and realize their import. He started to whirl around toward the others, a smile breaking, but he remembered to check himself in time. The face they saw as he completed his turn to them was implacable and Vulcan.

"Ship's message beacon."

Pike and Number One met the Vulcan landing party in the briefing room. Boyce had trailed along, his interest piqued by the unexpected find. The message beacon had been placed on the table and was still broadcasting. Its surface had been badly damaged, pitted and scorched, but the metallic voice uninterruptedly graveled on in an incomprehensible tongue, obviously repeating a message over and over.

"Ancient High Vulcan, sir," Number One said after listening intently for several seconds.

Six sets of Vulcan eyes snapped to her at almost the same instant. The look was approving. Pike studied her in some surprise.

"You understand it?"

"I *recognize* it," she replied evenly. "The old tongue is still used in a number of formal Vulcan ceremonies, but I do not understand the content except for a few words."

"Number One is quite correct, Captain." Spock moved forward a step and placed a hand on the beacon, thumbing a control on its underside. The metallic voice stopped. "Lieutenant T'Pris has recorded the message for our records. I believe I can give a reasonably accurate translation at this time. However, if you wish to wait for an exact word-for-word transcript—"

"I'll take your version of it now, Spock. We can cross-check it later for any discrepancies in the translation."

"Very well, sir. It begins with the call sign and name of the ship. The message was recorded by Captain Stepn. By the tone of the voice, I would say it was recorded hurriedly and under stress. The *He-shii* was breaking up as it neared GS391. The ship was doomed, and the few surviving crew members were abandoning her to take to a life shell. One of them was of clan Archenida, and he was carrying the Glory with him. They had decided to cast their lives in the hands of fate. The life shell would have had provisions and oxygen for ten occupants for three months."

"Warp capacity?"

The young engineer, Spahn, moved slightly, an alert expression on his face. Pike nodded to him. "Yes, Ensign?"

"Our ancestors did not have such a term, sir, but the life shell would have had a power drive that would give them the equivalent of Warp 2."

"So this life shell—something like a shuttle, I take it?" There were affirmative nods from the Vulcans. "The life shell would have been able to cover fair distances at low warp capacity for some time."

"Far longer than the occupants would have lived, if no suitable planet were encountered," Spock noted quietly. "Captain Stepn gave the course they intended to steer. He states in his message that he had decided to stay with the *He-shii.* I believe he meant for the message beacon to be ejected into space, possibly in orbit around GS391, so that it would be activated by the approach of any starship that ventured by. Unfortunately, several identifiable noises at the end of the message imply that the *He-shii* broke up even as he was recording, and the ship and the beacon simply fell to the planet surface in a flaming wreck. The beacon was activated by our presence, possibly by the workings of the tricorders."

Number One tapped the now silent beacon with a long, shapely fingernail. *Blue polish this week,* Boyce noticed. The first officer had decided tastes in cosmetic colors. The blue matched the intense hue of her eyes. "You said Captain Stepn gave the course the life shell was taking."

"He did, and I believe you will find it interesting. In our reckoning of the coordinates, their course was 32 mark 180 degrees." Spock let the information drop into their minds as a leaf dropped into a still pool, spreading gentle ripples.

Pike and Number One got it at the same time. "Areta lies directly on that course," Pike snapped.

Number One nodded and added, "With a three-month food, water, and oxygen supply and a sufficient warp capacity, they would have made it if they didn't deviate from that course."

"They would not have deviated," T'Pris said. "They had decided to accept their destiny as it came. The course, once chosen, would be kept."

Pike looked around at them—the Vulcans taciturn and waiting, Boyce cheerfully curious and interested, Number One neutral but with an alert intensity dancing in her eyes. "Number One," Pike said. "Take us out of orbit and set course for Areta at Warp 6. We had no reason to scan for spaceship debris on the planet before, or to ask about any mutants with pointed ears. This time we will."

Spock was seated in an attitude of meditation when his door chime pealed softly. He rose, frowning slightly as he turned. He expected no one. "Come in," he called as he pushed the hood of his robe back and down around his neck. The door slid open, revealing T'Pris.

"Oh," she said as she saw the formal robe. "I beg pardon. I did not realize you were meditating. I will call again later."

"No. Please come in. I was having some difficulty concentrating properly." He acknowledged ruefully to himself that it was not a prevarication. He had been having trouble keeping his mind in the correct state for clear meditation. He had received a formal message from T'Pring on the ship's personal message channel. To be absolutely correct, he had received a statement of her bride price, and it was high—fifteen hundred *nakh* a month. He hadn't especially minded that; the income from his estate would pay it easily. What had disturbed him was that when he had tried to bring T'Pring's face to his mind, he found it difficult to do so. He had perfect recall, but when he concentrated on a memory of her features, he could bring up only a vague, formless impression of an oval face with dark eyes, framed by dark hair—and no more. Yet he frequently found himself clearly envisioning the face of this woman before him—and not only her face but her body, her movements, her voice. Perhaps it was only her proximity, the day-to-day working relationship that had begun to develop between them, but he had worked with Vulcan women before, and none had ever hovered in his mind like this. He should be feeling the closeness of his betrothal link with T'Pring. Instead, he was haunted by this young widow to whom he had no more than working ties. He reflected ironically that he had *never* felt a link with T'Pring.

He gestured T'Pris toward a chair. *"Saya?"*

"Yes, please."

Spock went to the food compartment in the wall and spoke the order. In a moment, two cups of the steaming liquid were delivered in the small enclosure. He carried them over, gave her one, and sank into a chair opposite her, cradling his cup in his hands. "Was there something you wished to discuss with me?"

"I have been thinking of the Glory. Do you believe there truly is a possibility of recovering it now? Even if the life shell safely reached Areta, so many things could have happened to it, to them—"

"You are engaging in useless speculation. When we reach Areta, we will find what there is to find."

She sipped at the *saya,* her eyes fastened on the utilitarian carpet underfoot. "Of course, you are correct, Mr. Spock."

"Was that all?" He cursed himself for sounding too harsh. He had realized suddenly he didn't want her to leave.

"No. To be honest, I wanted to see what your life was like—in here. In private."

"Why should that interest you?"

To his surprise, she looked up at him with dark eyes that sparkled with just a hint of humor. "You are something of an enigma, Mr. Spock. You know

Vulcans can never resist an unresolved puzzle. You are one of us and yet not. You are reputed to be more Vulcan than any other Vulcan. Certainly, you are reputed to be more duty-bound to Starfleet than the most dedicated officer of any other race. Yet you seem so alone among other officers, alone even in the midst of other Vulcans."

He shifted in his chair uneasily. Without directly inquiring, T'Pris had managed to raise questions he would rather not answer. It was interesting to him that he was not offended by her asking. "I may seem alone to those who do not know me. I have friends."

"On Vulcan?"

"And in Starfleet. I am also"—he hesitated, then continued—"betrothed. I have declared the formal intent to marry."

"That is to be expected. But why is she not here with you?"

"T'Pring does not serve in Starfleet."

"T'Pring, of the family of Solen?"

"You know her?"

"*Of* her." T'Pris studied Spock a moment, then dropped her gaze. "When I brought Sepel's body back to his ancestral estate for burial, Solen, his daughter T'Pring, and his sons came to pay respect. She and her escort were courteous to me."

Spock carefully considered the statement. Vulcan women never gossiped; they floated quiet whispers, but whispers of truth. "Her escort—Stonn, I believe. His family has served Solen's house with honor for centuries."

"A shame you and she cannot be together," she finally said. "My husband would not have considered our marriage on any other basis." She allowed her eyes to rove over the copy of the ancestor statue from his family shrine which dominated one corner of the room, the traditional woven cloth in his house design which draped it. Bringing her gaze back to his, she said quietly, "I wept for a long time after he was killed."

"It is not seemly to show grief, T'Pris."

"Nonetheless, Spock, I wept." She set aside the empty cup and pushed to her feet. "Perhaps I am not the most Vulcan of all Vulcan women." She looked at him levelly. "I trust it will not spoil our working relationship."

"No . . ."

"I am sorry to have disturbed your meditation. I will not keep you further." He started to rise, but she held up a negating hand and quickly let herself out.

It was only after the door closed behind her that Spock realized that not once had they addressed each other as officers, but rather they spoke as friends. He pulled the hood of his robe up over his head and settled himself again on the floor mat to begin his meditation. T'Pris's face still floated on the viewscreen of his mind.

Arrival over Areta was routine and uncomplicated. Pike actually enjoyed seeing the predominantly yellow-brown ball growing larger and larger in their viewscreen as they approached at impulse speed and dropped into a standard orbit. He noticed that the harsher colors of the devastated areas of the planet were more softened by blues and greens than when he had been there before. Spock's verbal analysis confirmed Pike's notion that the two major city areas had begun to spread, encouraging the growth of trees and shrubs as well as irrigating more fields to raise crops.

"Start a planetary sensor scan, section by section, Mr. Spock. If the life shell got this far, there's a good chance it was able to set down somewhere."

"The *He-shii*'s accident occurred after Areta had suffered its own catastrophe, Captain, and before any major recovery of the planet's environment." Number One felt she had to point out the unpleasant possibilities. The executive officer frequently had that unhappy duty. "Even if the Vulcans were able to put the shell down safely, there may not have been any real chance of survival on this planet."

Pike nodded grimly. "I'm aware of that, perhaps more than anyone else here." The townspeople in the two cities that survived were fortunate in that they had prudently placed a number of key facilities underground before the holocaust. The nomads who survived did so in bleak areas that were not involved in the devastation. The mutants barely managed to stay alive in small groups and probably only because the gene damage they suffered made it possible for them to live in the hot spots the others couldn't tolerate. Gradually, the mutants had moved to the mountains and rallied there while the nomads held the deserts and the few oases close to the two cities. The life shell might not have had a choice about where it set down, and the Vulcans aboard probably had no inkling of Areta's history. If they survived, it might have been as mutants. If their descendants were found alive, it was possible they would no longer be recognizable as Vulcans. Pike glanced around at the silent, thoughtful bridge crew. "Start your sensor scan, Mr. Spock."

The tall Vulcan silently turned to his station and began to key in the elements for which the sensors would be scanning. Other bridge personnel went on with their routine duties.

It was three hours before Spock straightened up and turned back to Pike.

"Sensors are now picking up some scattered metal debris on the surface, definitely the alloy used in Vulcan starships and life shells."

"Position?" Number One asked quickly.

"Planetary coordinates—latitude 90 degrees, 20 minutes, longitude 130 degrees, twelve minutes. According to the planetary maps logged on the preliminary scan of this planet, this area is one of the most desolate sections of the great desert."

"On the viewscreen, please."

Spock hit a switch, and the map quickly appeared on the screen. Pike recognized it, having studied the entire desert area and the sparse concentration of nomadic tribes before his first trip down to the surface. "Not only desolate, Spock. It's still so wild that the nomads don't even frequent it. A little too close to mutant areas to suit them, I think. The only good thing about it is that there was very little fallout detectable when the first scouting ship did the preliminary scans."

"Didn't they do a full scan?" Boyce inquired from an unoccupied engineering station. "I'm surprised they didn't spot the metal debris."

Spock had been consulting his library computer,

and now he looked around at the older man in approval. "In fact, they did, Doctor. However, they appear to have assumed it was a relic caused by the holocaust. They did not scan the makeup of the metal itself; they only marked its existence on the surface, as they marked other devastation. They were looking for life, not metallic pieces of what they would call junk."

"Mr. Spock, take your landing team down."

"Yes, sir."

"And Mr. Spock?" The Vulcan paused to look inquiringly at the captain. "I hope you find it this time."

"May it be so," Spock replied.

The scene was almost a duplicate of the one on GS391. The landscape was different and far more barren. The mountains in the distance were saw-toothed, jagged in their youth, and unlike the ground-down molars of the smaller and older planet. But the landing party personnel were the same, and the trans-porter chief had once again set them down close to the largest detectable piece of debris.

It was recognizably part of an old Vulcan life shell. Pieces of it had been cut off and used to create several rude shelters. As the team slowly moved among the lonely relics, Spahn forged slightly ahead. Suddenly, he called out and pointed to a plot of ground a little behind the shelters.

"There, sir!"

The others, except for Spock, gathered around him to look where he was pointing. T'Pris let out a sad little sigh. The restless wind and the shifting sands had not been able to move the traditionally shaped rock cairns that had been built over seven bodies laid to rest there. The spitting hum of a phaser sounded behind them. Reacting quickly, they drew phasers and ran toward Spock standing rock-still in the encampment near one of the shelters.

"What is it?" Sefor called.

"How many did you find?" Spock asked, ignoring the question.

"Seven," T'Pris said. "That could not have been all, though. Who would have buried the last?"

"He was not buried," Spock replied quietly. "He stayed to do his duty. Here." Spock led them to one of the shelters. A makeshift door had been fashioned from one of the life-shell hatches. Spock had had to phaser it to be able to push it open. Inside the dim and musty interior stood a low table fashioned of rock and a slab of metal from the life shell. The desiccated skeleton of a Vulcan male lay stretched in front of it, as though he had lain down fully prepared to die. A container wrought of ancient silver in a geometric design sat atop the low table.

Spock looked around at Sefor and nodded to him. "You are the eldest. Please," he said, gesturing at the container.

The astrophysicist hesitated, then he stepped forward and slowly opened the lid. And gasped. "It is the Glory. Spock, it *is* the Glory! Finally." He reached in reverently with both hands and lifted the stone for the rest of them to see. Even in the weak light filtering into the shelter, the huge stone—the size of a large cantaloupe—gleamed in Sefor's hands. Then, sensing who the body at his feet must have been, he replaced the great emerald in its container. "He would have been clan Archenida, of course. By fate, he must have been the last to die, but even if he had not been, he would have insisted that he lie here with the Glory."

"I believe we will find you are correct, Sefor. We will look further in here to discover if any recorded message was left." Spock indicated two small, flat trunks set against one wall. "If there was, we will know the final fate of the party. If not, perhaps it is enough that it was we who found them and who will bring them home." He flipped open his communicator and said crisply, "Spock to *Enterprise*. Captain Pike."

"Pike here."

"We have found the remains of the Vulcans who escaped in the life shell, sir. We have also found Vulcan's Glory."

"Well done, Mr. Spock. Will you need any assistance down there?"

"Yes, sir. We will require a burial detachment to remove the bones of our honorable dead to the *Enterprise* for transfer to Vulcan and proper interment there."

"Security will have a crew down there in ten minutes. Anything else?"

Spock looked around at his compatriots. "No, sir. We will bring the Glory aboard ourselves."

Chapter Seven

PIKE WAS ALMOST CHEERFUL as he put together the articles he would take down to the planet surface with him. The question of the Glory had come to a successful conclusion. Starfleet Command was ecstatic at the message he had sent reporting the artifact's recovery. That done, Pike had very little more interest in it. He had examined the stone when Spock brought it to him and acknowledged with Number One and Phil Boyce that it was, indeed, a remarkable gem. It had almost dwarfed Pike's hands when he held it. Even uncut, its rough natural facets had glinted and glowed in the light, striking green sparks that enhanced its rich natural color. He had given it back to Spock with the order that it be placed in the security vault until they returned to Vulcan. Foremost in his mind now was Areta.

Well, he mused as he laid out a nomad desert robe, Areta was *almost* foremost in his mind. Janeese had been too much in his thoughts since he returned from leave. He welcomed the opportunity to get away from the ship, to beam down alone among strangers to execute a mission that, it was hoped, would see the townspeople and nomads of this civilization one step closer to a better life and a higher planetary survival rate. He was to look into the trade links they had made in the four years he had been away, to judge their progress. If it was healthy, as he hoped it would be, he had orders to leave it alone, and he would do so happily. If it had declined, his orders were still to leave it alone, but he would regret the waste and the loss of a civilization struggling to rebuild its world.

He was already wearing the close-fitting pants and shirt made of spun *ucha* hair. He sat down to pull on the high boots with tops that adhered tightly to his calves. The burnooselike outer robe would go over all, and, carrying a nomad's possessions bag and a water container, he would be ready to go.

As he rose, he caught a glimpse of himself in the mirror and paused to stare wryly at his image. He saw what Janeese had probably seen in him at first—an undeniably handsome and youthful man with an athlete's build and, when he was in uniform, a starship captain's stripes on his sleeves. Chris Pike wasn't an arrogant man. His looks had been striking from the time he was a toddler. He had discovered early on that a handsome face would not protect him from the hard knocks and disappointments in the world, nor would they help him in the fierce competition of Starfleet where he had cast his career. He had learned to rely on his mind and his instincts and the natural qualities of leadership he possessed and to dismiss the face nature had given him. Still, there had been women—one in particular who had meant much to him, but who had regretfully bowed out of his life because she was unwilling to be part of Starfleet and couldn't bear the idea of the long separations required by his missions. The other relationships had been impermanent, not taken seriously by either Pike or the women. Not that he had taken them lightly, either, but both parties recognized their impermanence and had let go without regret.

Janeese had been different. She had been introduced to him by mutual friends two and a half years ago when he had gone to visit his parents in Mojave. She was interested in becoming a Starfleet officer and became more interested in the career after they met. They approached each other warily, but they became lovers by the time his leave was over. While Pike had taken the *Enterprise* out on her next mission, Janeese had been accepted and started training at the Academy. He received frequent messages from her, filled with affection for him and enthusiasm for the Academy and Starfleet. Two years had gone by swiftly, and his leave this time had coincided with cadet vacation so they could meet again in Mojave.

Pike had not risen to the rank of captain without possessing an ability to read people. The minute he saw Janeese, he knew something was wrong. When he took her in his arms, he understood what it had to be. She was trying too hard to be warm and affectionate, and her body was stiff rather than pliable in his embrace. He had forced himself to keep his voice light and his smile gentle as he asked, "When did you meet him? Do I know him, or is he a classmate of yours?" The man who had captured Janeese's heart in Pike's absence was a Starfleet instructor, a desk man, not a spacer like him. Irony was something for which Pike had a philosophic appreciation. He allowed his appreciation of it to save him from bitterness and disappointment in Janeese. He was a caring and giving man by nature, and he had no desire to spend his life alone, with only the love of space and a starship in his heart. But he wondered often, and he wondered now, where was the woman who would gladly share that life with him?

Pike sighed, turned away from the sad-eyed captain in the mirror, and slipped on the outer robe. It fell loosely about him, and he belted it, arranging the folds in the overlapping style of the tribesmen. Already hooked on the belt was a sheath holding one of the sharp-bladed *dree* knives. A *dree* was a nomad tribesman's (or woman's) most valuable piece of equipment—weapon, utensil, and tool all in one. The possessions bag was rectangular and made of the tanned hide of the *ucha,* the gazellelike creature the nomads herded. Inside were personal items that might be found in any tribesman's bag. Pike's communicator rested in one of the deep pockets of his outer robe. The folds of the fabric would prevent it from being noticed, and the nomads' respect of person and possessions would keep anyone from accidentally discovering it. He had opted not to carry a phaser with him. The bulky water container in the shape of a pliable half-cylinder actually carried one of Pike's most important tools. A universal translator was sealed in a waterproof receptacle in one end of the container. It picked up the spoken word and translated it into Starfleet standard via a small bead microphone Boyce had implanted in Pike's ear. The captain had sleep-studied the Aretian language in the nomads' dialect before going on his first mission and reapplied himself to it before this one, and his command of it was reasonably fluent. The translator was a backup. It not only confirmed or corrected what he understood he heard, but it also offered suitable answers in Aretian if he needed to fall back on the prompting. Pike hung the water container by its short straps from hooks on his belt and slung the possessions bag on its long strap over his shoulder. Then he headed for the transporter room.

Lieutenant Commander George Meadows caught him in the corridor just outside Transporter Room 3. "Sir, if you have a moment?"

"Is it urgent, Meadows? Surely Number One or Mr. Spock can deal with any problems or questions . . ."

"This should come from you, sir, if you know what I mean."

"Frankly, Meadows, I don't."

Pike usually had only routine dealings with the ship's geologist. Though Meadows ranked Spock, the second officer headed up all science divisions on the ship and logically would be the person Meadows consulted. Meadows was short and thin and tended to be slow and economical in his movements. Pike had found the man's information on planetary geology and mineralogy accurate, detailed, and valuable each time he had called upon him. Meadows had always seemed a calm, even placid, man. ("Rather like his precious rocks," Phil Boyce had commented on one occasion.) Now, however, he looked anxious and tense.

"It's the stone, Captain—Vulcan's Glory. I'll need permission from you to study it." Before Pike could respond, Meadows rattled on, his ardor rising as he spoke. "An emerald that size is unprecedented. And it's reported to be virtually flawless, another precedent. This is the opportunity of a lifetime to catalogue it, measure it once and for all, holograph it for posterity . . ."

"No, Meadows."

"What? Sir?"

Pike shook his head. "I can't allow it. Vulcan's Glory belongs to them. You can apply to the Vulcan High Council through Starfleet channels for permission to catalogue and record it. That's as far as I'll go."

"But, sir, it's a geologist's dream."

"And an object of historical reverence for Vulcan."

"Sir, you have to understand . . ."

"Commander, the answer is *no,* and it is final. Is *that* understood?"

Meadows looked like a disappointed child, his face crumpling in near tears. "Yes, sir." He walked away stiffly, muttering half under his breath. "It's the opportunity of a lifetime. Geologist's dream . . ."

Pike watched him leave, then turned and punched a nearby wall comm, "Pike to Spock."

The answer came back almost instantly. *"Spock here, sir."*

"Spock, I'm ordering you to keep the Glory in the security vault until we can properly return it, unless we receive other orders directly from the Vulcan High Council. Clear?"

On the bridge, Spock curiously arched an eyebrow and glanced at Number One, who was seated in the command chair. The first officer arched an equally curious eyebrow back at him. What was this all about? *"Clear, sir. I will also relay your order to Security Chief Orloff."*

"Good. Pike out."

Pike turned back toward the transporter room and his interrupted mission. He beamed down into the desert under the friendly cover of night, as he had planned. No one had seen him; the nomads seldom stirred out of their camps after dark. Pike had chosen coordinates near the primary herding and grazing routes of the tribe with whom he had first made contact. Sensors had shown a fairly large group camped four kilometers away. In all likelihood, it was the tribe he knew, the one led by Farnah, a *shinsei* of great stature. Pike decided he would walk toward the camp directly after he beamed down. There was little chance of anyone questioning his comings and goings, but he wanted to leave a fairly well-marked trail for some distance, in case someone happened across it.

He had covered almost two kilometers before he felt confident enough to make his own camp for the night. Pike's possessions bag provided a personal tent of soft, compactly folded material that would ward off the sun during the day and keep body heat in during the chill desert nights. There were a few natural predators in the desert, but they were inclined to seek prey less combative than the tribespeople—or Pike. The smaller creatures that hunted in the night were no danger to him, and the tent was sealed to keep them out. He set it up swiftly, scooped out a comfortable hollow for his hips, pushed up a pile of sand for his pillow, and prepared for sleep. He could do nothing more until morning.

Pike dreamt of Janeese, clearly seeing her honey-blond hair as it curled softly around her face, creating a frame for her dark brown eyes, pert nose, and gently smiling mouth. She wore the dress she had worn when he asked her to be his, a gossamer thing in a shade of old rose, material that shifted and shaped and clung to her body sensuously. But that was wrong, because in the dream their friends were just introducing them, and she was looking up at him with an interested sparkle in her eyes that told him she liked what she saw. Someone was murmuring her name to him—Janeese Carlisle—and he felt himself smiling back at her, responding to her with an emotional jolt he had not felt for some time, unfamiliar but not unwelcome. Then the scene seemed to shift, and she was introducing him to someone, the instructor at the Academy to whom she had become engaged. She was pressing Pike's hand, dropping into his palm the friendship ring Pike had given her before he left on his mission. "Sorry, Chris," she was saying with tears in her eyes, her voice shaking. "I'm so sorry . . ." They were riding in the mountains on the two quarter horses Pike kept at his parents' home. Janeese was a good rider and handled her mount well. She was asking him questions about Starfleet, about the Academy, telling him her dream of venturing among the stars. She was looking at him adoringly as they rode side by side and saying, "With you, Chris. I want to be out there with you." She and Pike were curled together in bed, bodies still moist from making love, his hands running through her tumbled hair as he told her how much he cared for her. "I love you, too, Chris. I love you, I love you." And then she was shaking her head, sobbing, saying again, "I'm so sorry, Chris. I'm so sorry. You weren't here . . . I was lonely . . . Tom was a friend. A friend at first, and then more. You weren't here. I'm sorry. I'm sorry. I'm so sorry, Chris . . ."

Pike woke up sweating, and he abruptly pushed the folds of the tent aside to let in some of the cold night air. He sat cross-legged, staring out at the brilliant, star-flecked sky. Janeese had affected him more deeply than any other woman, had gotten in under the skin. Losing her—and in so mundane a way—bothered him a good deal more than he let on. He had walked away from her tears, casually pocketing the ring she had returned as though he had accepted her rejection. He sighed and admitted he wasn't as tough as he made himself out to be. Not about Janeese. That one had hurt deeply.

T'Pris had not planned to work late in the lab until a line of research inquiry had not given her the answers she anticipated. She stayed at her station, her curiosity piqued by the new questions raised, following where they led. She was concentrating so intensely on her screens and her science computer that the inquiring cough behind her surprised her. She whirled in her chair to find Meadows standing there.

"Sorry, Lieutenant. I didn't mean to frighten you." He didn't look especially apologetic, but then T'Pris hadn't been frightened, either.

"Is there some way I can assist you, Commander?" she asked politely.

"Maybe. Could I ask you some questions about the Vulcan's Glory?"

She eyed him neutrally, weighing it up in her mind that these were natural concerns of a geologist who also doubled as a mineralogist. The Glory was a legendary stone, and she understood Meadows had been denied the opportunity to study it. She nodded slightly, just once. Meadows promptly showered her with a barrage of questions about its diameter, its weight, its shape, the placement of its natural rough facets. She answered as best she could, but she finally lifted her hands in defeat.

"I am sorry, Commander Meadows. You desire too much technical information. I have no expertise in gemology."

Meadows pushed in closer to her, reaching out eagerly to almost touch her hand. She withdrew, uncomfortable with the human closeness of the man, but he ignored it. "Don't you see, that's exactly what I was trying to tell the captain. No one on this ship can research that stone, capture it on holograph and in a technical log, no one but me. *I* have the knowledge to apply. Surely you Vulcans don't deny the rest of the Federation a record, a mere *look* at the Glory?"

"I cannot say. It would be a matter for the High Council."

"On this ship, it's the captain's word that's law. If you could put in a good word with Pike for me, that would be all. You're a Vulcan and a scientist. Your word would mean a lot."

"I am sorry, Commander. Captain Pike has given explicit instructions for the security and handling of the Glory. To do as you suggest would offend my personal honor. It would be a defiance of the captain's orders."

Meadows stepped back, hastily apologetic. "Yes. Yes, of course, Lieutenant. You're absolutely correct. Captain's orders. A matter of honor. Naturally, you couldn't interfere. I'm sorry I intruded on you. Please forget I said anything at all." He half bowed and left her alone, scurrying out the door that just barely slid aside in time for him to clear it.

T'Pris stared after him thoughtfully, a small frown crinkling a V between her eyes. She turned back to her science computer and began to renew the line of research that had so interested her, but she found herself pausing again and again, considering the incident with Meadows and not liking it.

She finally set her research aside and went to Spock's quarters, but she hesitated outside the door. She had interrupted him once before. What would he think of her calling on him at this late hour? Still, she felt he should know of Meadows's approach to her. She was also an honest woman, and she admitted to herself that she wished to see Spock again, alone and off duty. She had loved Sepel deeply. They had been childhood playmates and friends all their lives. His death had left her alone and lonely for companionship for the first time in her memory. The year since his passing had been empty, except for the saving grace of her work. Spock, with the aura of mystery created by his half-human heritage, with his very correct manner, with his attractive mien, had touched her as Sepel had not. She frankly admitted to herself that Spock roused in her desires that her lifelong friend and husband had not. That surprised her and also pleased her. T'Pris reached out and touched the annunciator at the side of the door. Almost immediately, Spock's voice called out through the speaker, *"Enter."* The door slid open.

She stepped through the door and found him waiting for her. "Mr. Spock."

"T'Pris."

"Something happened a short time ago which I think you should know. It bears on the Glory."

"Tell me." He led her to the low couch in the sitting room area of his suite and politely waited for her to seat herself. "Something to drink?"

"No, not now. I thank you for the courtesy."

Spock lowered himself to the couch beside her. "What is it that disturbs you?"

"Lieutenant Commander Meadows came to me in the lab. He requested that I take his part with Captain Pike, that I ask that he be allowed to examine and catalogue the Glory. I told him that was impossible. He must know the Glory is sequestered in the security vault, as the captain ordered. The only change in those orders must come from the Vulcan High Council. I refused to assist him."

Spock studied her for a moment, their eyes locking. He nodded briefly. "Your actions were entirely correct."

She hesitated, then slowly said, "Yes."

"There is a problem you perceive."

"Not a problem. But it should be considered that perhaps the commander has an equally correct argument. The Glory is unique, precious, and possibly the most rare stone in the known galaxy. All he wishes to do is holograph and measure it, catalogue it for posterity, for the knowledge of the Federation planets. Can that be wrong, Spock?"

Spock hesitated, considering it. "No, not if that is the only thing Meadows wants. But he is a human. He is subject to a certain personal conceit, something that might even be called greed—academic greed. He is the ship's senior geologist. If he is the one to do the cataloguing, the holographing, the measuring of the Glory for the historical records, his name becomes associated with it. He may be asking for this permission for entirely personal reasons and personal gain, which is, perhaps, why Captain Pike has invoked the security requirements he has and why he has said only the High Council may change his orders. The captain is an intelligent and perceptive man. You were correct in refusing Meadows's request, as I have said."

"Then I have disturbed you for nothing."

"I was not occupied. When the chime rang, I thought it might be you."

T'Pris glanced away, almost shyly. "Why should you think that?"

"You have a way of knocking at my door when I have been thinking of you."

"Of me? Not T'Pring?"

"You also have a way of asking difficult questions."

She nodded, quietly acknowledging the fact. "So my parents said, and so said my husband. But now I am *T'Sai* T'Pris, *Aduna* Sepel *kiran*. For humans, a widow. For Vulcans, free to choose a new mate." She turned to look directly at him. "Or a lover. *That* is a difficult question to consider."

"I am betrothed," he said softly.

"But not wed," she said as softly. "Not yet."

Spock studied her for a long moment, considering what he knew of her, what he felt for her, the surprising emotions she called up in him. And he remembered what he knew of T'Pring, what he felt for *her*. The only emotions T'Pring brought forth in him were duty and obligation laid on him by others. Slowly, he reached out his hand to T'Pris.

Lightly, gently, almost fearfully, their fingers touched and caressed.

Night had fallen on the city of Sendai, wrapping its narrow streets in shadows. The twin moons of Areta had not yet risen, and only the stars lit a figure in black clothes moving quietly and stealthily from one pool of darkness to another. A few unshaded lamps still shone out onto the walks, making oblong slashes across the streets. As the figure in black slipped swiftly through one such slash, the light caught its face for a moment, revealing a handsome youth of perhaps eighteen seasons. His name was Bardan Aliat, and he was the heir and pride of the prosperous merchant Melkor Aliat. What he was doing now would certainly not fuel his father's pride but rather his outrage. It was late enough that the only people Bardan might encounter on the walks would be those who had tasted a little too deeply at the local drinks shop, none likely to recognize him.

His greatest fear of discovery came from the watchguards, who patrolled the high walls that circled the city on an irregular time schedule. Bardan, however, had taken the trouble to cultivate friendship with a young guard named Andor Clite and had learned his duty times. The great gates were still ajar, waiting for any last stragglers from the fields and the road to come in for safety. Mutants never came this close to the city, but they had in the Bad Times, and the townsmen never forgot it. There was still time before the Closing, but once the gates were locked for the night, they did not open for anyone or anything until morning light.

Bardan found shelter in an alley mouth in the street beside the wall and squinted up to make out the figure approaching along the walk on top. He could just see the watchguard silhouetted against the starlit sky. It was not his friend; it was the woman with whom Clite shared the watch. Bardan pulled back a little farther into the shadows and studied the street. It was wider than the ones he had traveled to reach this point. This was one used for the carts that moved their produce and merchandise to the markets. He would have to cross to the gate without cover. He reached under his jacket and brought out the timepiece his father had given him just two weeks ago. If Clite had been correct, he should be reaching this point on the wall very soon. He stared up again, saw the woman almost opposite him, and yes! Clite was recognizable approaching from the opposite direction. Bardan slunk back into the alley shadow until the two sets of measured footsteps merged as they passed each other and then separated again, moving away.

As soon as both watchguards had paced far enough past, Bardan ran for the gate on the balls of his feet, almost soundless. He had crossed only half the street when he heard one set of heavy ringing bootsteps suddenly stop. Why? Bardan could not pause; he pelted on, stopped gasping in the looming dark of the gate recess. He couldn't see from there what the watchguard was doing or which one it was. Had he been seen? If he had, why hadn't the watch raised a challenge? A townsman running out of the city at night was suspicious enough. He could bluff his way through somehow, saying he was restless and had come out to share part of the watch with Clite. Then he heard a striker and the distinctive *puff puff* of a *chooka*. Bardan let out his breath. It was Clite, who "suffered the vice" of smoking. The young watchguard had only stopped to light his pipe. The booted steps resumed their rhythmic pacing.

Bardan touched his hot face and found he was wet with a sweat so heavy it was streaming in rivulets. He mopped himself with a nose cloth, took a deep breath to steady himself. Clite's steps could still be heard going away. In the opposite direction, he could hear the faint sound of the woman returning on her rounds. Clite would be a little slower because he had stopped for that moment to light his pipe. Bardan had to go *now*. Quickly, he slid around the edge of the huge gate, paused in the recessed shadow of the outer gate portal for just an instant, and then quietly ran through the night. The giant *kerra* tree that stood sentry outside the gate hid him from view as the female watchguard solemnly paced by. Another moment, and she and Clite would pass on the wall, heading for the opposite ends of their duty round again. Bardan waited, shivering in the warm night as his muscles tensed nervously. The two watchguards met, crossed paths again, and walked on. Bardan left the protection of the thick tree bole and ran down the road toward the desert, the night wrapping its web around him. No cry was raised behind him. No one had seen him. He had done it!

Bardan hurried along the starlit desert road as fast as he could manage. He was in good physical condition, but he had seldom been out of the city at night, and the sounds that came ominously from so many places around him kept him in a state of constant tension. He found himself panting heavily and pausing often to look over his shoulder. The wind made a soft sighing over the dunes. There were night birds crying and other nocturnal creatures making strange noises. There was always the danger of mutants. He had heard of raids conducted this close to the city now and then, if the food in the mountains where they lived was sparse. He didn't know if it had been scarce recently, but he thought nervously that it *might* have been. He peered ahead and managed to make out the dark shapes of the *kerra* trees that formed a scrawny oasis here on the rim of the desert. That was his destination, but now that he had reached it, he hesitated. It was dark and still among the trees. Suddenly, the pale starlight of the sky overhead and the night noises that had disturbed him seemed much more friendly than that black stand of trees. He moved into it slowly, as silently as he was able. It seemed to grow darker as he came under the shelter of the thick-leaved branches. He held out a hand in front of him and promptly ran into the massive trunk of one of the trees.

As Bardan reeled back, startled, a shape suddenly leaped out from behind the tree and pounced on him. He shouted in fear as the robed and hooded figure knocked him to the ground and half fell on top of him, grabbing his wrists in a strong, fierce grip. As Bardan struggled wildly, he abruptly realized that the figure

holding him down was shapely and sweet-smelling—
and giggling uncontrollably.

"Silene!" he roared, angry now because he had been
caught in fear.

"Hush, hush," she laughed quietly. She put a hand
over his mouth lightly and rolled off him. "You are
soft yet, love. Not your fault. Wait until the desert
toughens you. Then I will never again be able to
surprise you like that."

He sat up, brushing sand off him, still pouting. His
eyes had begun to adjust to the dark under the trees,
and he could make out her lovely features, framed by
the material of her hood. He had no need of the light
to know she had long, thick chestnut hair and witch-
ing green eyes. The people of her tribe were all fair in
coloring, though their skin was always tanned brown
by the sun. She tilted her head mischievously, still
smiling at him.

"Forgive me?"

He wanted to pretend he was angry, but her smile
was prompting one of his own in response. Finally, it
broke across his face, and she launched herself into his
arms, knocking him flat again, but this time it ended
in a kiss that satisfied them both. When she raised her
head, she said solemnly, "I think I am forgiven."

"Most heartily forgiven," Bardan agreed. "But
Silene, we have to hurry. We're not that far from the
city. I wasn't followed, but if anyone looks in for me
after I supposedly retired to bed and they find I'm not
there . . ."

"Yes, love. You are right. We will need distance
between us and both our families. We will begin now."
She rose to her feet in the easy, graceful manner of the

nomad people. It was a move Bardan had never mastered. He clambered up after her and found she was holding out a hand to him. "Come. I have two *meercans* tethered here." She led him farther back under the trees, again smiling saucily back at him. "They are two of Father's best."

Bardan winced. "I suppose it was clever of you to take them, but he's going to be very angry."

"They were promised to the man who would bond me. Fortunately, no man had yet come forward, and I chose you as bond mate. The *meercans* are yours now." She reached the two saddle animals that snuffled affectionately against her sleeve. "Did you bring nothing to our bonding, love?"

"Well, my father has no *meercans,* and I couldn't carry much of his merchandise with me. I brought some food for us. And"—he jingled a pouch at his belt—"Father does have money. We can buy what we will need when we reach Andasia."

Silene flung her arms around his neck and nestled against him. "I have chosen a man of wisdom," she murmured.

The basic operating principle of the matter-antimatter engines of a starship was relatively simple, as so many brilliant ideas are. A dilithium crystal was suspended in the center of the injector core and subjected to a carefully directed stream of matter from the top of the core and one of antimatter from the bottom. The planes of the faceted crystal absorbed the two streams of matter that were deadly to each other and *redirected* them into a compatible river of material that produced warp power for the engines.

However, sometimes—not often, but sometimes—a little thing or two could go wrong. Nothing that would endanger the engines, or even the ship, but which could make a difference in the equipment involved in the operation of the system or anything attached to it.

The engineering graveyard shift was quiet as always. Scott had chosen this time to start through his first batch of engine-room hooch. The curiously shaped pipe-and-bulb arrangement that formed his still had been installed inconspicuously in a tangle of other pipes that hooked into the maintenance scope that looked into the injector core for routine inspections and servicing. As he had pointed out to Brien, no one had noticed it in the least, and it blended into the background of pipe and tubing that surrounded the core so naturally that no one was likely to. Scott carefully uncapped the maintenance scope hole, moved aside a neatly inserted (and nearly indetectable) circle in the wall of the scope hole, inserted a funnel, and began to pour in the mash and pure water that were the base of his recipe. There were other ingredients, which he measured out carefully and slipped into the tube in the wall. That done, he poured in more water, waited a moment, then took a careful sniff at the tube. The expression that passed over his face was pure bliss. His grandfather had told him you could always smell the quality of the end product in the first mix of the recipe, and Montgomery Scott's nose told him this would be a perfect batch. *Let them talk about the* Lionheart, he thought. *Wait until they get a taste of this brew!* He happily closed the scope hole and went back on duty.

At that moment, the dilithium crystal in the core

suffered an infinitesimal fracture along the edge line of a facet. Crystal fracture was one of the few inherent drawbacks to using dilithium, but it happened so infrequently (and every ship carried a number of backup crystals) that it was felt the risk was worth taking in exchange for the immense power possible through the system. This fracture was so tiny that only a microscopic investigation would have revealed it. With the warp engines in low idle while the ship was in orbit, it did not affect the efficiency of the crystal in transforming matter and antimatter into the correct mix of energy required. It did, however, result in a few stray gamma rays being thrown off in a direction not intended by the designer of the injector core. They bounced along the line of the maintenance scope hole and found the slightest edge of an opening in the side wall that did not inhibit their passage into the piping there.

The way had been long and arduous for the two riders in the desert. Silene had known the direction she was heading, guided by the stars, but Bardan had to take her leadership on faith. He trusted her; she was desert born and bred. But still, he had never turned his own life over to anyone so completely as he had to this slim young woman he loved. He had his moments of fear and vague doubts until the large *kerra* tree oasis loomed up before them, just as Silene had said it would. She smiled over her shoulder at him, and he could see that luminous look on her face in the light of the two moons which now shone high in the sky.

"Here we make camp," she told him as he urged his mount up beside hers. "No one will be here. This place is my tribe's winter graze, and they are south of Sendai now. They are not due to be here for months."

They moved into the shelter of the big trees and found a flat, grassy space near the center where a spring fountained into a sweetwater pond. Silene slid from her mount, handed Bardan the reins as he did the same, and told him to tend the *meercans* while she set up camp for them. Unaccustomed to being ordered, Bardan balked at first and then quickly realized her job was the more complicated. He tended the beasts quickly—unsaddling, watering, and feeding them. While he was occupied, Silene set out utensils, started a small sheltered fire in an old scooped-out cookpit, and assembled a meal that smelled wonderful to a man who had eaten little before beginning this adventure. She had also laid out sleeping rolls and had a full plate and cup ready for him when he rejoined her.

"I could eat a *meercan* on a spit," he told her with a smile. She stared at him, shocked, and he realized he had just violated one of the nomad's most sacred rules. No one spoke of a *meercan*'s death; the beast was too valuable to the tribesmen. The only way a *meercan* would ever be eaten by a desert dweller was if it was too old or too injured to be saved. The death of a *meercan* under any circumstances was a major loss to a nomad. "I'm sorry, sweet. It was a phrase, a townsman's phrase," he assured her quickly. "It means I'm hungry, that's all."

"You're sure?"

"Yes, Silene. I wouldn't *want* to eat a *meercan*. Really."

"I've made *ucha* meat stew."

He took a quick taste, then a larger one as the flavor burst on his tongue. "I like it. It's wonderful."

"Do you mean it?"

"I'll never lie to you, Silene." He set his spoon in his plate and reached out his hand to touch her lovingly.

She looked away, pretending to be withdrawn. "The wise women of my tribe say a man is already lying when he says such a thing to a woman."

"I come from a different tribe. I thought that was why you loved me."

"Oh, yes." The pretension was banished by her brilliant smile. Suddenly, their hunger was gone and the plates were set aside, and hunger of another kind overcame them. The bedrolls and blankets were close by, and it was only a matter of moments for them to spread them and find each other, touching and being touched, making discoveries they had not yet permitted themselves. They were so deep in their love, so lost in sensation, that they never heard the soft, padding footsteps that should have been their warning.

The creatures that leaped from the darkness, yanking Bardan away from Silene, were grotesque in the moonlight that filtered through the *kerra* trees. Bardan caught a glimpse of their faces and twisted, frightening bodies as they grabbed him. Mutants. He saw Silene fighting grimly, silently, trying to twist away from her captors to pull out the *dree* knife on her belt. Bardan tried to reach her as the mutants easily subdued her. She continued to kick and struggle until they bore her to the ground. Bardan shouted in rage and threw himself against the two mutants who held him. Strong as he was, they were stronger, and he was controlled as easily as a child. The mutants had him

128

and Silene trussed up and slung on their saddled *meercans*. They had their own mounts—odd animals something like *meercans* and yet unlike. Mutants also? The creatures' language was difficult to make out, but Bardan found, if he listened carefully, he could understand the gist of what they were saying. What he understood he didn't like. They were heading for the mountains the mutants controlled, the Druncara Range. No normal who had ever gone into the Range had ever returned.

Chapter Eight

PIKE WOKE TO A DAWN that was a soft glow on the horizon, rapidly spreading to a golden flood of sunshine. He made himself a cold breakfast of ship's rations and water as he sat on the sand and watched Areta's sun rise. From this point until he returned to the ship, he would have to eat as the people around him ate. Finishing the rations, he collapsed the personal tent and folded it neatly into his possessions bag. The tribe of nomads should be less than two kilometers south of him now, and he began to walk in that direction.

The desert wind that had blown most of the night had dropped to a whisper, and the sand lay still on the gentle dunes that dominated the landscape in this area. It had been a stroke of good luck that the first time Pike had beamed down and approached the tribe led by *Shinsei* Farnah, he had appeared striding out of the midst of a desert sand devil, a swirl of sand whipped up by the swiftly changing winds running ahead of a storm. The great nomad leader, Sadar-es, had come to the tribes in exactly the same manner, and Farnah's people had welcomed Pike generously because of the coincidence. Sadar-es had been a loner, something of a hermit, but either intuitive or learned enough to foresee the gathering trouble among the people of the planet that meant a catastrophic war. He had preached everywhere he went that the coming war would destroy them if they stayed close to the cities. The original tribespeople had then been little more than scattered individuals and groups who preferred to live off the land in the rural areas of their world, the rough equivalent of farmers and ranchers. More and more people had come to listen to Sadar-es as he spoke eloquently about the shadow of death that hung over Areta when the great powers that ruled the planet finally clashed in the war that would inevitably come. Many left the cities and embraced the philosophy the desert hermit preached. Before the final conflict descended on Areta, Sadar-es had led his followers deep into the desert fastnesses, where they had molded themselves into the nomad life now followed by their descendants. After the holocaust, Sadar-es had stayed with his people until they formed themselves into the eight tribal units that survived to the present. He saw them begin to organize their tribal government and taught them everything he had known of desert survival. He was calculated to be in his eighty-first year when he had abruptly taken up his possessions bag and water container and disappeared into the wilderness, never to be seen again.

The two cities that survived, Sendai and Andasia, had had leaders who also believed in the message

Sadar-es had preached, but they had no wish to give up their cities. Instead, they had begun to build down, burrowing into the bedrock beneath their cities and creating a safe shelter there. The townspeople had survived the holocaust by going deep and staying there until the surface environment was clean enough to support life again. Then they had emerged and started building *up*, beginning with stout city walls encircling their enclaves to protect them from marauding mutants as well as the tribespeople, whose nomadic ways they did not trust. Sadar-es was a legend among the city dwellers, too, a prophet whose vision saved them but also a renegade connected with the tribes. They were grateful for his warning and that their ancestors had heeded it, but they were just as happy he had disappeared into legend.

There were any number of tales about Sadar-es, one of them being that another prophet like him would come to the people to lead them in a new direction. Pike's appearance out of the sand devil had led Farnah's tribe to adopt a reverential approach to him, which he quickly worked to dispel. He insisted he was just a wanderer, content to live outside a tribe but needful of their company now and again. He told a story of originally being born to a tribe occupying desert lands on the other side of the planet, far enough away that his tale should go unchallenged. (His assumption was correct; Farnah's people never roved that far from their own established territory.) Pike told them he felt the need for solitude and meditation, and the nomads respected his story, asking few difficult questions. Pike had also carefully refrained from making any statements that might set him up as a potential prophet, but his shrewd direction in discussions of trade among the tribes had planted the seed of the idea that perhaps establishing mercantile contacts with the townsmen might be beneficial to all.

The tribespeople had successfully bred and herded their *uchas* from the beginning. These were hardy animals that needed little more than brush and scrub grass, some wild grains, and water to survive and multiply. The *uchas* provided milk, meat, long coarse hair that could be clipped off and spun into yarn, and hides for tanning. The nomads also cultivated the arts and crafts of leatherwork, weaving, pottery, jewelry of beads and desert stone, hunting, and a kind of hawking using a falconlike bird called a *torep* which they trapped and trained. They knew how to make food from the succulents, wild plants, and herbs of the desert and the oases. Their most revered weapons—*dree* knives, hunting spears, and swords—were relics handed down from before the holocaust, from father to son, mother to daughter. Firearms of any kind had apparently been set aside once the knowledge of how to create them and their ammunition had vanished. The disposition of a weapon after the owner's death was a serious matter and never lightly made. Their language was fluent and beautiful, often sensitive, and they could guide themselves by the sun and the stars, but only the *makleh* of the tribe could read or write or do sums. Pike equated the *makleh* with the tribe's secretary-treasurer. He or she did all the trading for the group; ensured that monies, animals, or trade goods were correctly paid and received; and recorded all agreements and all disposition of wealth through marriage or death.

The townsmen had controlled their subsurface environment since the holocaust and were beginning to exert some control over the ground near the cities. They had developed a viable, though limited, agriculture in addition to the crops they grew hydroponically and were also successful in raising small animals and poultry as well as a variety of edible fish in their ponds. They used wind and solar energy for power and obtained their water from the deep wells they had sunk. They had become sophisticated in weaving and dyeing fiber material from native *strella* plants and had developed a paper much like papyrus. They had stores of iron and copper and formed utensils and decorations from these metals, but alloys were beyond them, as well as beyond the nomads. The townspeople had maintained their education system, though many of the products and resources they had known in their history had been lost to them. It was considered unlettered not to be able to read and write, to master mathematics, at least one basic science, or one craft.

To any outside observer, the two groups could benefit from trade with each other, but first the initial barrier of distrust had to be hurdled. Pike had been able to act as a mediator between Farnah's tribe and the townspeople of Sendai by the simple expedient of suggesting the nomads set up a colorful camp outside Sendai's walls and open a bazaar as they would do among their own people at a tribal oasis. The townspeople had been wary of this activity outside their walls, until they had seen it was peaceful—and the food smelled good—and the merchandise seemed so very attractive and unique to their experience. A day

and a half later, Farnah and his *makleh,* Berendel,
welcomed a contingent of Sendai's leading merchants
headed by Melkor Aliat. The initial group was soon
followed by a larger one that discovered there was
room to deal and trade, with each side the better for
the barter. Pike had slipped quietly away that night,
knowing that communications lines were open and
the two groups were on their own and on their way.

Chris Pike mentally reviewed most of this history as
he trudged through the sand in the direction of
Farnah's camp, guided by the sun. He sighted the low
huddle of *ucha*-hide tents in the middle distance and
moved quickly toward them, expecting the warm
welcome extended to anyone who came to a nomad
tribe with an open hand and a peaceful heart.

What he walked into was chaos.

Farnah's voice was bellowing in anger and frustration from the main tent. Pike could hear the more
gentle tones of Farnah's wife, Ingarin, saying something else, only to be drowned out in another roar of
rage from the chief. A gabble of secondary male voices
chorused Farnah's outrage. Other tribesmen and
women huddled in groups, looking toward the main
tent, murmuring together in low tones, shaking their
heads. The *makleh,* Berendel, spotted Pike and came
toward him with the traditional carelessly graceful
hand gesture of welcome that moved from belt level
out to the right, ending with the palm up and open. It
showed that the greeter held no weapon to use against
the visitor.

"You grace us again, *Indallah* Krees." *Indallah*
meant "wanderer." He had used his first name, which

sounded more like a nomad name than his last. Berendel would not ask where he had been in the interim when he had not been seen. It would be up to him to inform her, if he wanted to. The smile on her face was genuine and attractive. Berendel was a striking woman, with sharp hazel eyes, fine aquiline nose, and sculptured cheekbones. Pike guessed she was somewhere in her forties, lean and wiry, her skin weathered by the sun and the wind.

"It is you who grace me with your welcome, *Makleh* Berendel," Pike replied. Another bellow of rage erupted from the main tent, and his eyes involuntarily shifted there. "I hope there is no trouble visited on the tent of *Shinsei* Farnah."

"Trouble and grief, friend Krees," Berendel said. "His daughter has disappeared in the night."

Pike's mind spun back over four years. He remembered that Farnah and Ingarin had five strong sons and one daughter. "The little sprite with the big dark eyes—Silene?"

"The joy of the *shinsei's* life," Berendel agreed. "And not so little now." She looked around as Farnah burst out of the tent and surged toward the tethered *meercans,* followed by his wife, his five sons, and their wives. "Come, you must see him now."

"He is distracted—"

"He will not become less so, Indallah Krees."

Berendel set off toward Farnah, and Pike had no choice but to follow her. She waved and called out to the *shinsei,* bidding him to see who had come to the camp. The big man looked around in anger, and his face twisted into something that was near a welcome when he saw who it was. Hospitality was important, especially toward one who had lodged in their tents before. He hitched himself around to face Pike and Berendel as the *makleh* led Pike to him. The others of the family waited on Farnah's response. With an effort, he made the welcome gesture, which Pike returned to him. "You grace us again," Farnah grunted.

"You offer me grace, *shinsei,*" Pike said politely. "I hear from Berendel that you have suffered a loss."

Farnah's anger rose again. "My child . . . my desert flower . . . my only daughter . . . kidnapped!"

Ingarin shook her head and stamped her foot, determined to be heard. "She has *not* been kidnapped, my man. Your sons have told you two *meercans* are gone from the tether line. There is no sign of a struggle, and only one set of tracks from our tent to where the *meercans* were tied. Every other member of the tribe is here, willing to take up chase after her. I tell you she has run off."

"Why should she run away from her home, her parents, her brothers?"

Ingarin glanced at Berendel in the timeless look that women share when they clearly want to shout, *"Men!"* Berendel dropped her eyes and pulled her head once to the right, half a negative shake, eloquent in its briefness. Ingarin turned back to Farnah, almost equal to her husband in size and certainly equal in her anger, now directed at him. "Why does any nomad woman leave her home? For a *man.*"

"What man? Name him!"

Ingarin poked Farnah in the chest. "Do you not

remember three grazings ago when we came near Sendai for the trading? Silene came to us, shyly, ashamed to tell us what was in her heart."

"She said she was drawn to a *town* boy," Farnah snapped, as if it were not worthy of his attention.

"And you raged in anger and forbade her ever to see him again."

Farnah shrugged, dismissing it. "She agreed she would obey. What of it, woman? Silene has been content to do her duty as daughter of this house ever since."

Ingarin shot another glance at Berendel and one at Pike, looking for support. "She *said* she would obey. She *seemed* to be content. But we are a half-day's travel from Sendai and a new trading, and Silene—"

"Has been kidnapped by that upstart cur!"

"Silene has run off to meet him. Or perhaps some other, though I doubt that. We cannot know her heart, but whoever she went to, she went voluntarily. I risk the good of my word on that."

"The tracks seem to say our mother's words are true, Father," one son ventured.

Farnah turned on him angrily, still unable to accept that his precious jewel of a daughter could do such a thing. "Then this boy has used Silene's innocence and trust to persuade her to run away with him. To *ruin* her and leave her. These townsmen are not to be trusted." He glared at Pike, and the captain hoped fervently that Farnah did not remember that Pike had subtly encouraged the traffic between town and tribe.

Berendel moved slightly, a gesture toward Pike. *"Indallah* Krees has come from the direction Silene appears to have taken, *shinsei*. Perhaps he has seen something."

Pike quickly reviewed the look of the terrain he had hiked over. He had seen no tracks leading out toward him until he had neared the encampment. "I camped two kilometers from here when night fell, *shinsei*. I was tired and fell asleep soon after dark. I heard nothing in the night, but perhaps weariness took hearing from me. I saw no tracks when I came to you until I came on some *meercan* trail back there." He gestured over his shoulder.

"Asleep and heard nothing, eh? It is easy to die in weariness if mutants or other marauders are about, friend Krees."

"I will sleep lighter in the future, *shinsei*."

"Enough. We will trail the *meercans* and catch up with my disobedient daughter and this boy, if that is who is with her. You spoke with those trademen, Krees, did you not?"

"When first you went to trade, yes."

"I have never spoken with them. But perhaps you and Berendel can deal with them if need be. We must get Silene back."

"I'll do all I can," Pike said quietly. The girl had surely complicated things—the boy, too, if Ingarin was correct that it was a plan the two of them had hatched. But if the girl could be brought home none the worse for the adventure—or if some suitable resolution could be worked out—perhaps the promising trade agreements between Farnah's tribe and the Sendai townspeople might not be jeopardized. Strangers were welcomed into the tribe and often through marriage. But Pike did not know who or what the boy was or his motives, and his welcome might be dubious at best. If the young man could not adapt to the tribe, he would be cast out, and Silene would be shamed. Her shame would rebound on her father and cost him honor, possibly the leadership of the tribe.

Although the wind had blown much of the night, it had been fairly gentle, and the *meercans'* tracks were deep. The partially filled-in hoofprints were still clearly visible to trackers with the experience of Farnah and his sons. Ingarin was left to follow on with the other families and the herds. Berendel and Pike mounted *meercans* and accompanied the main group of trackers which would travel far more quickly.

At first, the tracks headed almost directly for Sendai, as Farnah expected. There was no discernible trail leading from the city to the nomad encampment, and it seemed to prove Ingarin's contention that Silene had taken the two *meercans* ("Farnah's best," Berendel had confided to Pike) and gone to Sendai to meet someone.

Then the tracks began to veer to the east, away from the city. Farnah deliberated over them with his sons and included Pike in the conversation.

"Perhaps someone else stole the mounts and Silene as well," the youngest son, Neepah, suggested.

"But you say no one else is missing from the camp," Pike pointed out. "And these tracks say no one came from the city for her."

There was a nod of agreement all around. Finally, Farnah's eldest son, Durlin, spoke up. "Father, if we continue in this direction, we will end at Antorin Oasis."

"I see it in the trail," Farnah agreed. "But why should Silene ride to our spring encampment if she was to meet the town boy?"

"It *is* within walking distance of Sendai," Berendel pointed out. "A safe meeting place for both, perhaps?"

"Silene was lured there," Farnah said with finality. "Great promises must have tempted her there in spite of my orders."

Berendel murmured quietly to Pike, "Great promises or perhaps great love."

"You are often the matchmaker for the tribe, *makleh*. Do you believe in love?"

She smiled slightly. "The girl was of an age to be bonded, and several young men were interested in her. No one spoke of love, only of the size and value of her dowry. Silene spoke to her mother of her caring for the town boy. Why do *you* think the girl has gone?"

"I think you're quite right."

It was midafternoon, a quiet time on the *Enterprise*. She held steady in standard orbit, no navigation required, very little monitoring of instruments. Meadows was counting on the peaceful ordinariness of the day to assist him. He was taking a huge risk but one he justified to himself as absolutely rational and entirely called for. The security man at the vault appraised Meadows as he approached. Meadows recognized him as Security Officer Reed. This could be difficult. Meadows had been hoping for a less experienced officer, but he intended to carry his plan through nonetheless.

"Good day, sir," Reed said politely.

"Hello, Reed," Meadows said casually. "I've come for the Glory."

Reed shot a curious look at him and frowned, but Meadows was already offering him the clipboard he carried under his arm. "Captain Pike's authorized me to evaluate and document it for the library-computer records. You know, measure it, weigh it, holograph it, that sort of thing."

"Yes, sir, I understand." The security guard examined the authorization clipped to the board. The captain's signature was clear at the end of the order.

Meadows felt a bead of sweat roll down his chest and hoped his face wasn't perspiring as noticeably. He had worked for hours on the signature, carefully copying it from departmental orders Pike had previously signed. The scrawled "Christopher" was lumpy and descended from the initial clear letter into a wavy line. "Pike," however, was written strongly and firmly, as though the surname meant more to the writer than the given one.

Reed looked up again and smiled. "Everything seems to be in order, sir." He turned and, shielding the electronic combination from Meadows's view, entered the number and letter series that would unlock the vault. The heavy door swung open, and Reed stepped inside the big safe. He appeared a moment later with the Glory in its carrying case. "Here you are, Commander Meadows."

Meadows took it, thanked him, and started to turn away. "Commander." Reed's voice stopped him in his tracks. "How long do you think it will be before you return it? I'll have to put it in my report."

"Oh. Oh, yes. I would say three hours to do the job

properly, but it might take longer. That's all right, isn't it?"

"Certainly, sir." Reed smiled and gave him a friendly half-salute. "Just be careful with it."

"That goes without saying, Officer Reed." Meadows walked away, balancing the heavy carrying case in his left hand. The Glory was his, for a little while, anyway, and he could hold it and examine it with no one else to interfere. That was all he wanted. But once it was done, Pike would see the value of his study of the stone. Meadows was absolutely certain the captain would not waste his effort insisting that the evaluation be eradicated. The captain would understand that Meadows was entirely justified in what he was doing. Entirely justified.

Dr. Philip Boyce lazily leaned back in the reclining chair that molded gently to his body and stared at the ceiling of his sickbay office in pleased rapture. The good feeling had something to do with the shot glass in his hand. He glanced at the chronometer and grunted. The timing was perfect. He reached out to the ship's intercom button on his desk and tapped it.

"Boyce to Bridge."

"Number One here. What is it, Doctor?"

"You have exactly one minute to the end of your duty shift, correct?"

He could almost see the first officer frowning slightly, wondering what he was up to. Her voice came back noncommittally. *"That is correct, Doctor. And if you know that, you didn't call me to ask for the time."*

"You are correct. Next question from you is, Whaddaya want? Also correct?"

"An inelegant phrase for you, but accurate."

"I am about to satisfy your curiosity. When you come off shift in"—he checked the chronometer again—**"ah**, thirty seconds, I'm inviting you to drop by sickbay to participate in a scientific experiment of great importance."

There was a pause, then her voice said, *"I'm surprised you don't feel Mr. Spock would be more suitable for such an experiment."*

"Sorry. He'll have to wait for his promotion. Only first officers qualify for this one. Are you coming?"

There was a slightly longer pause than before. *"I will be relieved in exactly five seconds, Doctor. Then I'll be down."*

Boyce grinned cheerfully at the intercom. "I'll be waiting." He tapped it off and relaxed back in his chair. He had one eye on the chronometer, mentally counting off the minutes, and had reached five when the sickbay door slid open to admit the executive officer. She glanced around at the unoccupied beds and then crossed to the door of Boyce's office to look in at him. Her eyes shifted from his face to the glass he held. "About this scientific experiment of great importance?" she asked.

He raised the glass to her in salute. "First batch of the new mission."

A smile lifted the corner of her mouth, and her deep blue eyes softened slightly. She stepped into the room and comfortably hitched one hip up on the edge of his desk. "It was kind of you to invite me, Phil."

"Chris and I usually christen the first wringings together, but I thought you might like to join me in his absence." He hooked another shot glass from the cabinet behind the desk, poured out a half-measure from a beaker, and handed it to her.

"You're being a miser with that."

"Wait until you taste it before you judge your fellow officer. *Skoal, prosit, à votre santé,* down the hatch."

She chuckled, lifted the glass toward him in a toast, and took a sip of the waterlike liquid. Her eyes widened as she swallowed, and for a moment the white-hot sear of it down her throat held her speechless. Boyce looked at her benignly. When she could manage it, she gasped, "What is *in* this?"

"Good, huh?"

"Good is not the word, my dear doctor. More like—ambrosia. Nearly lethal until it gets to your stomach, but ambrosia after that." She looked deeply into the glass with great respect. "Warming, too. Who's responsible?"

Boyce studied the glass he held, considering the question. "Well, we've never had a batch like this before. Stands to reason it's a new man. What do you think?"

"Hmm. Most likely an engineer. Two or three new ones this trip." Number One took another cautious sip of the brew, held her breath as it burned its way down. "You know, this is better than the *Lionheart's*."

"I wonder what's in it."

"It has been my experience, Phil, that when it comes to engine-room hooch, it is often better not to ask."

"Oh, well, in that case, drink up."

They solemnly tilted their glasses together, tapped rims, and did exactly that.

* * *

Farnah's party reached Antorin Oasis in the late afternoon. As they entered the shadow of the *kerra* trees, they heard voices at the center of the grove, near the deep pool that welled there. Pike saw several pedal vehicles standing just inside the oasis. The tribesmen quickly dismounted and moved forward, hands on the *dree* knives at their belts. Pike and Berendel followed just a little behind them.

The men standing at the pool were townspeople. Pike recognized one of the prominent merchants he had met four years before, Melkor Aliat. Aliat was as tall as Farnah, but with nowhere near the same bulk, a strong man but soft with town living. He had an aristocratic face, a thick mane of gray-flecked dark hair and intelligent brown eyes. As he saw the nomads approaching, he turned on them angrily.

"So you've come back to the scene, have you? Where is my son? What have you done with him?"

"Your son?" Farnah snapped. "We have no concern for your son." He turned to Berendel and Pike. "Speak to this one."

Aliat moved in on Farnah, ignoring the others. "Bardan was forbidden on pain of death to see the nomad girl." He snorted disdainfully. "The boy is young, gullible, believing he loved her. I thought it was settled and done months ago when I ordered him to forget her. But last night he left the city, and we followed his trail here. This is your oasis, *Shinsei* Farnah. Was it your girl who lured him?"

"Lured him!" Farnah roared. "Silene would never—"

"Your people kidnapped him—"

"Never—!"

146

Pike and Berendel pushed in between the two shouting fathers, separating them gently, careful of their dignity. *"Shinsei* Farnah, Trader Aliat, please. A moment to speak quietly." The two men backed off a few steps, glaring at each other.

"Good men," Berendel said in a conciliatory voice, "surely there is some agreement to be reached here. I am *makleh* of *Shinsei* Farnah's tribe, but I see there are two sides to be considered here."

Pike had conferred briefly with Durlin, who had rejoined the group after scouting the oasis and studying the ground. Now he turned to the two fathers. "Two sides indeed. *Shinsei* Farnah, your own son has examined the tracks. The thing that is clear to him is that Silene brought two *meercans* from your camp to this oasis. Another person—we will assume it is Bardan—walked here from the direction of Sendai. Two persons rode out together, away from the city."

"It is true, Father," Durlin said. "You may study the evidence yourself. The ground has been walked over by these townsmen here in the oasis, but the tracks in and out can be easily read."

Farnah and Aliat glared at each other, angry and stiff in their assumptions. Pike exchanged a glance with Berendel and nodded at her to speak. "The two must have met here by agreement, good men. There was no kidnapping. They have run off together."

"Then your son plotted this!" Farnah snapped at Aliat. "My daughter is pure, naive."

"Pure? Bardan is shy, inexperienced. He has no idea of the desert. It was your daughter who—"

"Good men! Good men, *please!*" Pike interrupted. The two men subsided, glaring at each other but grudgingly listening to Pike. "There is no blame attached to either of you. I think these two young people decided they loved each other and that their parents were wrong to demand that they stay apart. So they got together. Whether they love each other and should be married is a question to be worked out." Farnah and Aliat both grunted angrily at the same time. Pike shook his head. "You are rightfully concerned with their welfare, but nothing can be done until they are found. Let me go after them and bring them back to you. Surely they will both see that running away from their families and their duties is not the best beginning for a marriage—if there is to be one. It is up to you, their fathers, to speak through the *makleh* about a correct, acceptable marriage bargain." He paused and looked at the two men. They were glaring at each other but seemed to have calmed a little.

Farnah turned to Durlin. "In what direction do the tracks lead from here?"

"Toward our winter graze at Tisirah Oasis, Father."

"Mmm," Farnah grunted. "Silene keeps to the places she knows will provide them with water and shelter." He looked at Aliat. "What say you, Trader Aliat? Shall we let *Indallah* Krees bring our children to their senses?"

"Yes," Aliat snapped. "But I'm going with him."

"So am I."

Pike winced. Alone he might have been able to convince the two youngsters that they should come back and seek out a suitable marriage agreement in accordance with custom. With their fathers at his heels, the young couple might be far more difficult to deal with. *"Makleh* Berendel, will you come with us? I think there may be need of your services as a mediator."

Berendel bowed her head and touched her palms together lightly. It was a symbol of acquiescence and agreement to the suggestion. Only Pike saw the expression on her face, the half-smile and twinkling eyes that told him she realized this was going to be a touchy, but amusing, situation.

T'Pris moved her knight to the second level of the three-dimensional chess game and looked over the board at Spock. He nodded, approving the move which put one of his bishops in danger. The long, slender fingers of T'Pris's right hand crept along the top of the table beside the board and caressed Spock's left. He captured her hand in his and raised it to his lips, the game forgotten. Their duty tours were over for the day; there was a long night to follow.

She smiled at him and rose, tugging him with her. As one, they moved to the bed. She reached up to playfully dishevel his shining dark hair with the ruffle of bangs that started over his brow. He started to move to straighten it, but his hand involuntarily went instead to the coil of braid that crowned her head, and he found himself unfastening the pins that held the braid in place. She allowed him to free the braid and helped him loosen the thick hair that hung to her waist. She shook her head, and the curtain of hair cascaded around her winsomely. They moved sideways together, instinctively found the bed, stretching out on it. Smiling, his eyes half closed in lazy anticipation, Spock held up his right hand, fingers spread, and

T'Pris matched it with her left. The tactile contact sent a flow of warmth through him. Their eyes locked, and the look went deeper, mentally chaining them together. He sent the first gentle probe along the bond, reaching out to her.

T'Pris opened herself to him, welcoming him, the merging of their feelings racing after the intimate mind touch. He felt her glory in the flickering touches he sent along her most intimate nerve endings. She began to tremble in anticipation and joyously sent back the same. The simple fingertip-to-fingertip touch shifted as he grasped her hand fully, fingers winding together tightly.

Her mind touch became bolder, more sensual, under his encouragement. He felt her hesitation about probing too deeply yet, a little afraid of her full Vulcan abilities matched to his. He sent another caressing thought along the bond, urging more from her, wanting to feel the full envelopment when both minds were open and responsive. Just as the delicate touch of her *sensitive* reached him, the desk comm wailed with the traditional bosun's whistle, and Number One's crisp voice spoke.

"Mr. Spock, please report to me in the geology lab immediately."

Spock's hand tightened on T'Pris's briefly, then he rose and tabbed the intercom. "I will be there in five minutes."

"Very good. Number One out."

Spock turned to T'Pris, his eyes warm and gentle and promising. "Whatever it is, I will hurry to be done with it."

"I will wait."

"Wait just as you are now."

Catlike, she stretched her lithe body on the bed and smiled at him. "As you wish, master of my heart."

Spock felt an emotional shock that plunged from his chest to the pit of his being, and his breath caught for a moment as he stared at her. The phrase was traditional, exchanged often between husband and wife and between betrothed lovers. T'Pring had never used the phrase to him. T'Pris meant it; he could see it in her eyes, a look of love that was soft and gentle and forever.

"I will return as soon as possible—mistress of my heart."

"I accept your word as a promise," she said gently.

Spock hastily put his uniform to rights and left.

The geology lab was not very familiar to Spock. He had not yet had an opportunity to work closely with the scientists and technicians there. When he arrived, he found Number One and Dr. Boyce waiting with Security Chief Orloff. Another man hunched timidly near the lab door, as though afraid to stay but forced to. Spock glanced at all of them curiously as he entered the lab, but before he could ask why he had been called, the first officer stood aside and gestured behind one of the work tables.

Lieutenant Commander Meadows was sprawled on his back on the deck, his eyes staring at the overhead lights. Spock immediately realized that the man was dead. His eyes flickered back to Number One.

"Meadows told his lab technician, Sandson, he wasn't needed on duty this shift. At first he took the time off, but Meadows's order bothered him, so he looked in on the lab fifteen minutes ago and found him like this."

"Not a natural death, I assume."

"You assume right," Boyce said flatly. "Meadows was murdered."

"Why?"

"That is the question we're here to investigate, Spock. The man was innocuous, inoffensive, a scientist who tended to his business almost to the exclusion of everything else. Who would want to murder him, and, as you ask, why?"

Chapter Nine

SPOCK CAREFULLY SCANNED the geology lab, then brought his eyes back to Orloff. "There seems to be no sign of a struggle."

"Suggesting Meadows knew his assailant." The security chief nodded. "I noted that, too."

"Since no one has beamed onto the ship, it has to have been a member of the crew," Number One said grimly. "I don't like to think about the implications of that. Starfleet doesn't normally harbor murderers in the ranks."

"An act of passion, perhaps?" Spock ventured.

"Meadows never seemed to have any, except for his rocks," Boyce commented dryly.

Number One turned to him. "Never mind the sarcasm, Doctor. Have you determined the cause of death?"

"Oh, yes. Quite simple. Meadows was strangled."

Spock glanced at him quickly. He had had only a cursory look at Meadows's corpse, but suddenly he felt the intuitive flash of what humans called a hunch. "Pardon me, Doctor. Do you mind if I examine the body?"

"No, of course not."

Boyce stood aside as the Vulcan knelt beside Meadows's corpse. Spock leaned close to study the man's throat, carefully tilting the head to one side to examine the neck column.

Number One noticed and pushed forward a step. "Something?"

"This man was strangled in a very particular way, Number One."

"Explain, please."

"I am speaking of a Vulcan method of killing."

Number One's eyebrows arched upward skeptically. "Is that possible? I understood Vulcans to be a peaceful and uncommonly logical people."

"Now they are," Spock said. "In ancient days, we were warlike, savage. There are several hand-to-hand killing methods that were practiced. One was *tal-shaya,* the breaking of the neck. Another was *lan-dovna,* strangulation by one hand. It is still taught in Vulcan self-defense techniques. One does not wish to expect a killing attack on Federation planets, but one goes . . . prepared to defend oneself."

"Meadows didn't strike me as someone who'd attack a Vulcan," Number One said pointedly.

"No. But attack or defense is not the question. It is the method we have under scrutiny. I have never before seen a victim of *lan-dovna,* but the evidence is unmistakable."

The executive officer turned inquiringly to Boyce. "Do you concur, Doctor?"

"I don't know anything about this technique Spock's talking about, but yes, the marks are plain on Meadows's throat. Only one hand was used to strangle Meadows. The right hand, if you're interested."

"Can anyone other than a Vulcan do this *landovna?*" Number One inquired.

"I do not believe so. Certainly no one else on this ship." Spock paused, then went on doggedly. "I must tell you that Vulcans of both sexes are trained to accomplish this feat by the time they are adolescents. The most likely suspects for this murder would include all Vulcans on board."

"I see. Thank you, Mr. Spock. You've been most informative. Commander Orloff and I will undoubtedly be calling on you again for assistance."

"I must point out to you that I am also a suspect."

"Noted."

Orloff pushed his way forward, feeling neglected in this discussion. "We have to inform the captain at once."

"No." Number One shook her head and then held up a hand in the face of Orloff's protests. "We're under strict captain's orders not to communicate with him on the planet surface. To do so might place him in danger, or at very least might put him in an embarrassing situation. We must wait for him to contact us. With that as a given, I will conduct the murder investigation until such time as the captain can do so himself."

"Motives, Number One?"

"Your guess is as good as mine, Commander. Until we discover one, we'll have to operate on the idea that the murder was for unknown reasons, possibly unpremeditated. We will sequester and question all Vulcan personnel on the ship until we discover the murderer."

T'Pris turned to Spock, smiling softly as he entered his quarters. She realized something was wrong when she saw his grim face. "What is it?"

"Lieutenant Commander Meadows has been murdered."

"Murdered?"

"Approximately two hours ago, by Dr. Boyce's estimation. Rigor mortis had not yet set in. The body was only just growing cold."

T'Pris lowered her eyes in sympathy, thinking of the earnest man who had so urgently entreated her to put in a word for him with the captain in regard to the Glory. If Meadows had had selfish motives for making the request, he still had wanted it to further Federation knowledge of a great Vulcan artifact. "He was a good geologist. I did not know him well, but he seemed to be an efficient scientist, a capable officer . . ."

"I know, T'Pris. But there is more. He was murdered by a Vulcan."

"No. That could not be."

"There is no question of it. The murderer used *lan-dovna.*"

She stared at him, horrified. "But that is taught only in self-defense. Meadows could not have attacked anyone. He was not a physical person. It would have been laughable for him to attack a Vulcan for *any* reason."

"Nonetheless, it was the technique used. There was

no sign of a struggle, of an attack. It appeared to me as though Meadows was the one attacked."

"Why would anyone—least of all a Vulcan—wish to murder him without provocation?"

"I believe Number One and the security chief will be giving that question the most serious consideration. But . . ." He paused, and a gentle smile curved his lips. "I also believe it will be a while before they call you and me for questioning." He reached for her, and she smiled back, sensuously running her fingertips up the palm of his hand.

Number One and Orloff immediately set up a preliminary interrogation of the seventeen Vulcans. None of them except Spock and T'Pris appeared to know the reason for the questioning. As luck had it, all of them had been off duty at the time of the murder. Every one of them contended that he or she was alone at the probable time of the murder, except for Spock and T'Pris, who admitted they were together. Number One lifted an eyebrow at that information but accepted it equably otherwise. Starfleet had no strong rules about fraternization between officers, and personal affairs were usually kept personal. T'Pris was a widow; Spock was not married. Number One would not condemn a relationship between them, unless she discovered it was a cover for murder.

She turned to the screen mounted on Orloff's desk and called up the personnel file on T'Pris. Almost as soon as it was displayed, Number One said, "She's clear."

"Why do you say that?" Orloff asked.

Number One tapped the screen display. "T'Pris is

left-handed. Most Vulcans aren't, but a small percentage favor the right brain. Boyce was positive the murderer was right-handed, which lets her out."

"Could she be ambidextrous?"

"No. According to all Starfleet testing, she is totally left-handed."

"She and Spock claim to have been together most of that evening. Would she cover for him? The relationship appears to be . . . close," Orloff said discreetly.

Number One debated with herself and finally nodded. "She might. But is it conceivable that Spock is a murderer?"

"He's half-human, Number One. Maybe that cuts the conditioning, makes him vulnerable to passion. She said Meadows approached her earlier in the evening. What if she told Spock something that roused his anger—or his jealousy?"

"Perhaps." Number One considered it and finally rejected it. "Every notation on Lieutenant Spock says he embraces a code of nonviolence that would simply preclude his being a murderer. He is also the one who pointed out the exotic strangulation technique that neither you nor I would have easily detected. I just don't believe it is possible, Orloff. And what would be his motive?"

"It's the motive that puzzles me in the first place. We know Meadows was a fine scientist in his field but a nonaggressive man by nature. Not one to pick a fight—if a fight *can* be picked with a Vulcan. What could have precipitated his murder?"

"I'm not a detective," Number One said quietly, "but I like to read mysteries, especially the classics. I'm not sure I'm quoting correctly, but I believe Sir

Arthur Conan Doyle had Sherlock Holmes say something to the effect that when all obvious possibilities have been exhausted, the only possible answer is the *impossible*. So, while it seems impossible that a Vulcan committed murder, it also seems impossible that anyone *other* than a Vulcan committed the crime."

"Including Lieutenants Spock and T'Pris?"

"Somehow I find it difficult to include them. They swear to being together. Unless I discover some other clue that would link them to the murder, I'm inclined to dismiss them from consideration. There are still fifteen other Vulcans who are suspects, Mr. Orloff. None of them can account for themselves except on their personal word, and all of them admitted to being able to perform the killing *lan-dovna* technique. I'm afraid we're committed to discovering who among them killed Meadows—and why."

Pike had been wondering to himself how he had managed to be at the head of this strange troop of gypsies on the way to the Tisirah Oasis. He had offered to lead a search for the two straying children of *Shinsei* Farnah and Melkor Aliat, convinced that the young people had simply eloped and would soon be found happily together and defying their parents' conventions. Then it would be a simple matter of their facing parental anger and effecting reconciliation. Somehow, the string of people who insisted on accompanying him along the trail left by the two youngsters had multiplied into Farnah and his sons, Melkor Aliat and his attendant friends, the following nomad tribespeople, and all their animals. Pike was not ungrateful for the tracking services of the nomads, but the trail was so broad and clear that even he could have followed it without real trouble. The long cavalcade that meandered after the tracking head of Farnah and his sons was worthy of a crusade.

He looked back at the muddle of people and animals ambling along behind them and frowned. Berendel, riding beside him, noted it and smiled quietly. "Something troubles you, *Indallah* Krees?"

"I think you understand what has happened between these two young people, *makleh*. Rebellion against what their parents decreed and a chasing after their own hearts. That's between them and their elders. Who are all these others who seem to have an interest in the matter?" Pike sighed wearily. "Why do these things have to get so complicated?"

Berendel smiled slightly. "You have little experience in the ways of dealing with people, I think." Pike shot her a sharp glance, one engendered by his years of command. Though she could not know that was behind the look, she shook her head and amended her statement. "Not people. You have dealt with them—I see that in you, Krees. Perhaps it is the emotions that you do not quite understand here. As a *makleh,* I see all these things in making a barter, a will, a marriage. It is always the high feeling that will tell in these dealings, the loves and the hates, the suspicions and the trust. When emotions run so high, there are many who must be interested in them, because they will win or lose by the decisions that are made."

"And in this case?"

"Ah. Silene is the last child of her father's loins, the only daughter. He thinks of her as his desert flower, pure and sweet as those flowers are. She is only seventeen seasons, and he cannot believe she can possibly have the urges of a young woman who wants her own man. Another difficulty—the young man she wants is not acceptable to Farnah because he is a town boy. Aliat is a merchant of importance. Bardan is his only son, his heir, and Bardan is moved to love a nomad girl. Unacceptable to Aliat, despite the emotions and desires of his son. Now, who gains if both these wayward children are disowned by their fathers? I have bargained for my people with Aliat, and I know there is a stepson who assists him in his business. It is likely this boy would come into more inheritance if Bardan is disowned. *Shinsei* Farnah's daughter has a sizable dowry that would go to her brothers if she were shamed and cast out by her father. I do not say that any of this will happen, but it could. All those who follow us are here to see what will happen. Greed and curiosity are common failings among us, yes?"

"Common to many beings, I think, *makleh.*"

Berendel nodded to indicate ahead of them. "Tisirah Oasis," she said. "Perhaps we will find these children now and make a settlement of this thing."

Before Pike and Berendel reached the outer edges of the *kerra* tree grove, they heard the wail of sorrowing tribesmen. "What's happened?" Pike kicked his *meercan* to greater speed and entered the shade of the thick trees. As he drew up, he could see Farnah's tall bulk in the center of the oasis, pacing up and down in a frenzy. Aliat was on his knees beside the pool, beating his fists on the ground. Pike dismounted quickly, dropping the beast's reins so it would stand obediently in a ground hitch. Berendel followed him, sliding off her *meercan* with the instinctive grace of the nomad.

"Shinsei Farnah, what is it?"

The big man flung out a hand toward the pool and the ground beside it. "My daughter is gone beyond saving. The tracks tell all—there!"

Pike and Berendel moved closer to the poolside, where Aliat knelt in sorrow with Silene's brothers. The youngest, Neepah, looked up at them and gestured toward the personal possessions scattered beside the water where a camp had been set up. The rumpled blankets lay beside the ashes of the fire that had died. Even Pike could read the signs of the struggle in the remnants left on the ground, and the tracks in the soft earth at the edge of the pool were unmistakable. Bardan's and Silene's were regular and small beside the twisted, gross prints that studded the ground.

"Mutants," Neepah said sadly. "Silene and the town boy were camped here. The beasts came out of the dark and carried them away."

"Where? What direction?"

"Toward the Druncara Range."

"Why should the mutants come here?" Pike frowned, studying the situation carefully. "This is very far from the Druncaras. The mutants don't come such distances lightly."

"You are correct, friend Krees," Berendel said. "I have not heard of them approaching so close to us or to the townspeople in many years. There is something strange about this."

Melkor Aliat rose to his feet, tears running down his cheeks. "My son is lost. Lost forever."

"Perhaps not, Trader Aliat," Pike said. "These tracks seem very clear and easy to follow."

The others stared at him, blank and silent. Durlin shook his head sadly. "There is no hope of saving them, friend Krees. The mutants kill their captives. It is said they . . . that they eat their flesh. Our sister is dead, and the foolish town boy with her."

"You will pardon me if I don't accept that as a pure fact," Pike snapped irritably. "You've given up before you have even tried."

"But it is useless."

Pike turned toward Aliat and Farnah, who stood together, joined for this moment in grief for their children. "I would like a moment to myself—to meditate on this great sorrow that has visited you."

"As you will," Farnah responded. He gestured deeper into the grove of *kerra* trees. "There is quiet there and peace for meditation." He looked around as the van of the followers began to arrive at the edge of the oasis. "I must tell Ingarin of our loss."

"I'll come with you," Aliat said suddenly. "It's my loss, too."

Farnah studied him briefly and nodded. "Yes. It is no comfort, but we both share the sorrow. Come then, Trader Aliat."

Pike watched the two men move away, leaving the group beside the pool. "I will be a while in meditation, *Makleh* Berendel."

"Do you think you will find an answer to this tragedy?"

"Perhaps. I don't know, but I will try." Pike walked away, picking a path among the trees of the oasis that would move him out of sight of the nomads. When he was far enough away, he reached inside the voluminous pocket in his robe and pulled out his communicator. Flipping it open, he waited for the cheerful *pip* of its active signal and then said, "Pike to *Enterprise.*"

Number One glanced up quickly as the communications officer swung around in his seat toward her. "Captain Pike, Number One." She tabbed the communications button on the chair arm and snapped, "Number One here, sir. I'm very glad to hear from you."

"Trouble?"

"Yes, sir. We've had a murder on board."

"What?"

"Lieutenant Commander Meadows was killed several hours ago—"

"Number One, if this is a joke . . ."

"Dead serious, sir. That's not a pun."

"Motive?"

"I'm sorry, sir. That's one of the things we're investigating right now."

Pike's sigh was audible. Number One could picture him shaking his head in frustration as he said, *"You'll have to handle it for now, Number One. I have a double kidnapping down here to deal with. The son of one of the merchants and the daughter of a nomad leader have been taken by mutants. I have to try to get them back, alive and whole. If I can do it, the alliance between the townspeople and the tribes just might be saved. I want a Vulcan and a couple of other alien crew members to beam down to assist me—"*

"Negative on the Vulcan, sir. All of them are under suspicion for the murder."

"Vulcans? All of them?"

"Well," Number One amended, "except for Lieutenants Spock and T'Pris. We've cleared T'Pris, and she claims she and Spock were together at the time of the murder."

"Do you believe her?"

Number One turned it over in her mind, remembering what she had said to Orloff in their discussion of the matter. "Yes, sir. I do. I don't believe Spock could have been the murderer. That's just a gut feeling, you understand, but I'll stand on it. I'll send Spock and two other aliens down to you in twenty minutes."

"Make it ten, Number One."

"Yes, sir."

"Do you have enough help to continue the murder investigation?"

"Affirmative. In addition to Commander Orloff, I'll enlist Lieutenant T'Pris and Dr. Boyce to assist."

"Good. Now, listen to my instructions carefully. Spock and the others are to beam down wearing particular costumes and in a very specific place. I'll give you the coordinates . . ."

Farnah and Aliat huddled together beside a cook fire, ignoring the others around them, refusing food, sharing a grief universal to parents. Melkor Aliat, widowed many years, was grateful for the little niceties Ingarin offered him in comfort. She was insistent that he have a bit of tea, that he sit with them to wait for Indallah Krees. Neither man was hopeful, but somehow Ingarin kept a brighter view. She sometimes felt women had to take a different outlook for the sake of their sanity, that there was light on the other side of darkness, that for every loss there was a gain, that for each tragedy there was some hope to counterbalance it. Ingarin had placed her optimism on the wanderer. She didn't know why, but she had always sensed a purer strangeness about him than just the tale he told of being a loner.

"He has been longer than he said he would be in meditation," Aliat said fretfully. He stood up to peer into the deeper darkness of the oasis trees.

"Meditation is one with the man. Who can say how long it should take?" Ingarin said quietly. "It is as long as it needs to be."

"Yes, of course. It is not my way, but I understand you have the right of it, madame."

She smiled a little shyly at him, liking him for the honorific. "My name is Ingarin, Trader Aliat. If our children are in love as they say they are, perhaps we should speak as friends."

Aliat looked away as Farnah pushed to his feet in agitation. "Silene is not a city woman. She would never be happy behind that boy's walls."

"Perhaps not, my man. But the boy may be happy in our tents."

"No," Aliat said quickly.

"It is not for you—either of you—to say. It is for them," Ingarin pointed out calmly. "And if we do not gain them back, our ideas of what they want are for naught."

Pike reappeared among the *kerra* trees, and Farnah saw him first. *"Indallah* Krees is here." They waited for him to approach, and he smiled encouragingly as he neared them.

"I've decided I will continue after the mutants and bring your children back if they are still alive. If you'll both come with me, or delegate others to come with me . . .?"

"No, it is not possible," Aliat said. "My men and I are not outside-born. We know nothing of the desert and the mountains. We would only be a drawback to you."

Pike turned to Farnah and saw the big man pulling back inside himself as much as the townsman. The *shinsei* had no excuse as valid as Aliat's, but he shook his head firmly. "There is no use to going, *Indallah* Krees. No one—*no one*—comes back from the Druncara Range. Not alive. Sometimes bones have been found, left as signposts to mark the mutant lands. Our children are lost forever."

"I tell you they certainly will be if no one tries to save them. And you who love them, even you will not go with me?" Pike stared challengingly at Farnah and Aliat, and the two men dropped their gaze away from him.

"I see. Very well. I will go."

Ingarin pushed her way forward. "You cannot go alone. A large band of men might have a chance, but not one by himself. You will also be lost to us."

"I do not propose to go alone." Pike turned, shaded his eyes against the bright desert light that beat against the cool of the oasis, then pointed. "They'll go with me."

167

The others turned to see three hooded and robed figures trudging through the desert sands toward the oasis. They moved purposefully, striding across the ground, looking neither left nor right at the nomads and townsmen tending *meercans* and crouched around small campfires.

Pike held up an arm and called out to them. "To me. Here." They moved unswervingly toward Pike, finally stopping before him and executing deep bows. Their heads were completely shrouded by the hoods of the desert robes, and their faces could not be made out.

"We have come to serve you, *Indallah* Krees," one of them intoned deeply.

"Who are these men?" Farnah asked.

"Not men," Pike replied. He gestured to the three, who reached up and pushed back the hoods to reveal their faces. Those who could see them gasped and involuntarily took a step away.

"Mutants!" The word rippled among the onlookers, softly at first and then louder as it reached the outer edge of the group. Instinctively, some of the nomads reached for their weapons.

Number One had sent Lieutenant (j.g.) Endel, the reptilian Kelyan, Lieutenant Ars Dan from engineering, a short Dioptan with a reddish complexion and a gnarled, troll-like face—and Mr. Spock.

Pike flung up a hand and looked around at the Aretans. "These are my friends. They'll go with me where you will not—and with luck and grace, we will find the two children you value."

Farnah and Aliat exchanged a look, saying much within it. Clearly, the wanderer commanded these mutants, and if that were so, it might be that he actually *would* be able to recover Silene and Bardan. "Friend Krees, we will camp here and wait for five days for you to return. If you have not come back by then . . ."

"If we haven't returned by then, you will know we are dead. But I expect we will be back in less time than that, *shinsei*. We'll bring your children—or their bodies—back to you. I promise it. Do we go with your blessing?"

Farnah nodded. "The grace of life and hope go with you, *Indallah* Krees," he said quietly.

"From all of us," Aliat added.

Pike bowed to the fathers and Ingarin. Then he turned, gestured to his three crewmen, and began to walk away from the oasis, toward the Druncara Range which loomed darkly in the distance.

Chapter Ten

NUMBER ONE paced the top level of the bridge, frowning in thought, turning over the problem of the murder. Orloff was reinterrogating the Vulcans one by one, but his brief reports to her had all been negative. The bridge watch glanced over at her from time to time; none of them spoke to her, not wishing to disturb her concentration. The lift doors slid open behind her, and she swung around to face Security Officer Reed as he came off the elevator.

"Number One, I just heard about Commander Meadows."

"Yes? What's your interest?"

"Well, I wondered about the Glory."

"What exactly did you wonder, Mr. Reed?"

The young security officer looked around, plainly worried. "You see, ma'am, the commander came to get the Glory, and I released it to him, but now—"

"What do you mean, you released it to him?"

"He had the captain's signature on an order to allow him to examine the stone. You know, for scientific purposes. He said he'd return it in three hours or so when he'd finished with it. But he hadn't brought it back when I turned over my duty shift to Lieutenant Bryce. I didn't think too much about it, because he said it might take longer. But when I went down to the rec room, I heard the commander had been murdered. So I wondered, what about the Glory? It should be returned to the vault, don't you think?"

Number One sighed heavily. "It should if it were in our possession, Reed. You'd better come with me. Commander Orloff and I are going to want to hear all the details on this."

Orloff examined the clipboard and authorization Reed had given him, finally shook his head. "Obviously a forgery."

"Not too obvious a forgery, commander, or Reed wouldn't have been taken in." Number One had studied the signature purporting to be Pike's. After a moment, she said, "It looks to me as though Meadows might have copied the captain's signature from routine ship's department orders. He did it well enough to get past a cursory examination, which is all Officer Reed here could be expected to give it under the circumstances."

Orloff glared at her, then at Reed. "There were strict orders to keep the Glory in the security vault unless other orders came through from the Vulcan High Council."

"True. But Reed was on duty at the vault and couldn't have known then whether or not the captain had reversed that order. The post is tucked off in a corner, with only one man assigned to it each shift."

"It's a lonely station," Reed agreed.

Number One nodded. "And here, apparently written out and signed by the captain, is an order to release the Glory to a scientist of the ship for good and valid reasons. If I'd been on duty, I probably would have accepted it, too. Reed might be faulted for not conferring with you before he let Meadows take the Glory, but even you might not have questioned a written order from Pike. Meadows was taking a chance that the order would come under some scrutiny, but not too much. The man seemed to be obsessed with the stone, wanting to study it, even against captain's orders. He contrived to get hold of it. That was his crime."

"But why murder him?" Orloff asked. "What was the harm in his examining it for the record?"

"The Glory is a national heritage, an historical artifact of great importance not only for its actual value but for what it means to the Vulcan people. Perhaps one of the Vulcans on board learned Meadows had violated the captain's order, took offense at him handling it . . ."

"I could accept that if Meadows had been challenged, perhaps even beaten up for what he had done—but *murder,* Number One. Why murder the man for his trespass? And, more important, where is the Glory now? We went over that lab from top to bottom for clues. There was no sign of the stone."

Number One shook her head, sighing. "I don't know. All I know is that Meadows's murder and the disappearance of Vulcan's Glory are tied together—and a Vulcan on board this ship is the criminal."

Pike, Spock, Endel, and Ars Dan followed the distinctive mutant animal tracks until they were well out of sight of the oasis and anyone who might have followed them. Berendel and Farnah had trailed them for a short way, urging the use of *meercans* on them until Pike had had to accept the animals. He had not intended to have to deal with the mounts, but the only way to stop Farnah from continuing to follow them with good advice was to take the proffered animals and ride away. When they had gone far enough to be clear and had checked their back trail for any shadowers, Pike waved the group together and dismounted. The others followed suit, and Endel gathered up the reins of all four *meercans*. "Tether them over there," Pike said, pointing to the side of the trail. There was small shelter in the shade of several *kerra* trees there, and Endel led the *meercans* to it. Pike flipped out his communicator and contacted the *Enterprise*.

Number One was not on the bridge, but the third officer was on duty. She responded quickly. *"Enterprise. Oyama here, sir."*

"I need a sensor scan for any life-form clusters in the Druncara Range. If you need coordinates, the planetary mapping scan will give them to you."

"One moment, sir. We're scanning for you now." There was another moment of silence, then Oyama's voice came clearly over the communicator. *"There is*

a large concentration of life forms in the high treeline of the central massif. Possibly a village or an encampment."

"Nothing between where you are reading me now and that reading in the Druncaras?"

Silence, then Oyama replied, *"No, sir. That is all."*

"Good. Four to beam to a point within one kilometer of that concentration of life forms."

"Yes, sir. I will give the coordinates to the transporter chief now. We will put you down in an area east of the life-form concentration. Sensors show trees and rock formations there that will offer some cover so you will not be seen beaming in. Enterprise out."

Pike looked around at the others. "Whatever the mutants plan for Bardan and Silene, they wouldn't risk doing anything to them here on the flatlands. They would have headed for their refuge in the mountains, and I doubt they stopped until they reached it. The encampment or village—whatever it is our sensors are reading—is the most likely place to find our two runaways."

"We have been delayed in discovering where the victims were taken, Captain," Spock pointed out. "If the mutants are as savage as they are reported to be—"

"Possibly even flesh eaters," Ars Dan put in.

"Possibly so," Spock agreed. "If they are that savage, sir, we may be far too late."

Pike nodded, acknowledging the possibility. "Bardan and Silene could be dead. I hope not. However we find them, I've promised to return them to their parents."

Suddenly, there was the distinctive high hum in the air that signaled the beginning of transportation. The four officers positioned themselves in preparation for it. A glittering, sparkling glow covered their bodies, shimmeringly outlined their shapes for a brief moment, and then slowly dwindled to nothingness. The high hum faded away and left the desert silent except for the soughing wind.

T'Pris asked to see the murder scene after Number One delegated her to the investigation. There was no reason why she should not, and the first officer opened the sealed lab for her scrutiny. Boyce and Number One followed her in, wondering what she might see that they had not. She wandered through the lab, carefully studying everything. She stopped beside the science computer on the lab table where Meadows had worked and activated it. She ran a quick check of its files, then ran it again. At the end of ten minutes, she turned to Number One and Boyce, frowning.

"Well, Lieutenant?"

"There is nothing tangible, Number One. But there is something else, an intellectual feeling I have."

"Feelings?" Number One smiled at the younger woman. "I didn't think Vulcans admitted to such aberrations."

T'Pris tilted her head and allowed a brief curving of her lips. "I said an *intellectual* feeling." She paused, trying to pin it down. "Something does not fit into the mosaic we are putting together here."

"How so?" Boyce asked. "I think it's pretty clear on the evidence. A Vulcan apparently murdered Meadows using a known Vulcan killing technique. Whether it was premeditated or not is in question. Meadows had the Glory in his possession. The Glory is gone. Presumably, the Vulcan who murdered Meadows took it."

"Yes," T'Pris agreed. *"Presumably. Apparently.* But in spite of the many circumstances that seem to say Vulcan, there is something *non-*Vulcan here. I admit only a Vulcan is trained to use the *lan-dovna* technique and has the strength to use it successfully. It is possible a Vulcan could have learned of Meadows's appropriation of the Glory and interpreted his handling of it as an insult or even the violation of a sacred relic of our people. Vulcans have a highly developed sense of justice. The murderer might have been moved to avenge that sacrilege if it was interpreted as such."

"Aren't we saying the same things?" Boyce asked.

"No."

"Explain, please," Number One said.

T'Pris lifted her hands in a helpless gesture, shaking her head slightly, trying to explain the un-Vulcan elements that were troubling her. "Even if such a thing happened, the Vulcan who committed the crime would be forced by honor to turn himself in for punishment. To take someone's life even by accident is so deeply against the code we live by that there would be no other action possible for a true Vulcan. We have yearned for the recovery of the Glory for so long. Now that it has been found, taking it for personal gain would be unthinkable. The person who murdered Commander Meadows and stole the Glory is hiding behind lies. No Vulcan would do that."

"But you admit it *had* to have been a Vulcan who committed the crime."

"It would seem so. I have no explanation for the dichotomy, Number One. I only know it exists, and it puzzles me completely. And there is something else."

"Yes?"

T'Pris turned toward the science computer on the lab table. "If Dr. Boyce is correct about the time of death, Commander Meadows apparently had the Glory in his possession for almost two hours before he was murdered. His reason for getting it in the first place was to study it, record all its aspects, holograph it for Federation records. He must have used this computer to do at least some of the preliminary work, but no record, no files of any kind, exist that indicate he did so. That seems to say those files were erased by the criminal. Why?"

Number One nodded. "Good question, Lieutenant."

Montgomery Scott came off duty ready to turn in, but Bob Brien had other ideas. When Scott entered their quarters, Brien was counting up a stack of credit chips and smiling happily over the tally on his pad. "Scotty! Glad you're back. Time to get to work."

Scotty headed straight for his bunk and collapsed on it. "I've *been* at work, man. D'you not see the chronometer? I've been an extra two hours on shift recalibrating the starboard impulse engine."

"Never mind about that. Look at these orders we have to fill." Brien leaned over him, pushing the pad in front of his face.

"Don't know why she slipped out of calibration like

that," Scott mumbled. "Might've jumped too fast to warp after she came out of drydock . . . maybe too high a warp . . . didn't take enough time . . . to run her up to speed before . . ." His eyes slid shut.

Brien dropped a handful of credit chips onto his roommate's chest. "C'mon, Scotty, wake up." Scott pried open his lids and groaned. "We have customers to satisfy." Brien's mischievous blue eyes sparkled happily. "They want more of that hooch. I checked our stock, and we can fill about half the orders now, but you'll need to start another batch through."

"Later," Scott moaned, flopping over on his side. "I canna do it now." He tried but couldn't stifle a body-shuddering yawn. "Later . . ."

"Scotty, you don't understand. Our customers are clamoring for the product *now.*" A snore rose from the bed, reverberating richly in the quiet room. Scotty was dead to the universe.

Pike led his small team through the trees and tumbled rocks that stubbled the mountainside. The Druncara Range ascended from the plain in a series of ridges that were thickly wooded on the lower flanks, thinning out to skimpy rock-strewn slopes at the tops. The transporter chief had set them down about halfway to the top of the third major ridge. Most of the trees were heavy-boled and resembled those of the evergreen family, though there was a scattering of deciduous trees and a variety of bushes, grasses, and mosses on the lower levels. The treeline was just a little above them, and there was still enough cover for the men to move freely toward the coordinates which sensors had pinpointed as a probable mutant settlement. They did come across a stone-fenced mountain pasture in which strangely formed animals grazed. These were oxlike in body formation but with three eyes and what appeared to be dromedary humps in the center of their backs. One particularly large specimen was penned away from the rest of the small herd, possibly a bull. The beast snorted at their approach and watched them warily until they had passed by.

Spock had been using his tricorder to get a triangulation on the settlement and now gestured forward. "Life forms ahead of us, Captain. Probably on the other side of that rise."

"All right, let's split into two parties here and take a look at the situation. Endel, Ars Dan, you make a sweep to the left, and we'll take the right. We'll meet back here in fifteen minutes."

Pike nodded to Spock, and they headed on an angle up the slope. A few minutes later, they were belly down, carefully parting some brush at the crest of the rise to peer down into the valley below. They saw a well-established village, composed of artfully designed buildings of mortared stone. Family homes were graced with porches and verandas that sported heavy growths of vine as shade curtains. The streets were unpaved but of hard-packed earth that obviously saw a lot of traffic.

The hill on the opposite side of the valley had been terraced, and small fields there were under cultivation. A stream tumbled and shouted down the hill on that side to spread into a pool at the foot of the slope. Pike could see a well-made bucket and pulley mechanism that lifted pool water up the terraces to irrigate the fields.

The people they could see moving about the streets and working in the gardens were performing perfectly normal tasks, but even from this distance their appearance was hideous. Few of them looked alike. All had malformed bodies—too many limbs or not enough, and some of these were strangely shaped. The faces that could be seen were warped and inhuman, a terrible contrast to the handsome nomads and townspeople from the flatlands below.

"Looking at their way of life here," Pike said thoughtfully, "makes me wonder if the mutants are as savage as everyone thinks they are."

"They do show a talent for building and agriculture, sir. Still, history has shown that many races even more sophisticated than this were capable of the cruelest savagery. They *did* kidnap Silene and Bardan."

Spock lightly touched Pike's arm and pointed a long finger to the left. The building was on the edge of the village and not very different from the others, except for the mutant who appeared to be on guard in front of it. A female mutant approached the building, carrying a heavy basket covered with a cloth. She paused beside the guard and lifted a lacquer-ware box from the basket. The guard allowed her to pass into the building with the rest of her burden. The man sat down and opened the box to reveal a selection of small delicacies that he began to pop into his mouth with gusto. Five minutes passed, then the door opened, and the woman reemerged carrying a different basket filled with empty dishes.

Pike signaled Spock to retreat back down the slope, and they paused at the bottom to confer in low voices. "A guarded building. A number of dishes of food going in and out," Pike said. "That has to be where they're keeping them prisoner."

"A logical conclusion, Captain. It is possible the mutants could have some criminals of their own held there, but more than likely it is the two we are seeking."

"Now, all we have to do is get them out." Pike looked at Spock, who stared back noncommittally. "My grandmother used to say everything is easy with the mouth. It's the *doing* that's hard."

"An excellent observation, sir."

"I have an idea, something like an old Indian trick."

"Did it work for the Indians?"

Pike searched Spock's face. Perfectly serious; he was not making a joke. "Yes. Frequently."

"Ah. Then I suggest we rejoin Lieutenants Endel and Ars Dan and plan the details."

Number One and Commander Orloff faced the squads of security officers and engineers in the large briefing room with the battle plan they had worked out. The Glory had to be on the *Enterprise;* therefore, the entire ship had to be searched from disk top to keel bottom. The 'tween decks service passages and Jefferies tubes would be examined with a fine-tooth comb, and the engineers would open up any areas that promised a hiding place. Anything that even hinted at being a potential concealment for the Glory would be investigated.

Scott and Brien, seated together, exchanged a horrified glance. "It'll have to be moved," Scott whispered frantically.

"We *can't*. We have too many orders to fill. Maybe they'll look the other way if they happen to notice it."

"Not while Number One's in charge of the search. The chief engineer won't be *able* to ignore it."

Brien glanced around to be sure he wasn't overheard, then he hissed, "We have to keep it producing up to the last possible minute and then move ahead of the search teams. We'll double in behind them when they've cleared out and reinstall it."

"I canna just be carryin' the thing through the corridors as it is," Scott snapped. "It's too big. It'll have to be broken down and reassembled and *then* reinstalled."

One of the other engineers leaned forward to poke his head between them. "Quiet, you two. I'm trying to hear the exec."

Lieutenant Pete Bryce had raised his hand and caught Number One's eye. She nodded to him. "Bryce?"

"I understand we have fifteen suspects. If their quarters are going to be searched, what are we going to do with them while we conduct it?"

"Commander Orloff is handling that."

Orloff briskly stepped forward. "All suspects will be held in detention cells while their quarters are searched. They will be returned to house arrest when the search teams are through in those areas."

T'Pris had been given the difficult assignment of informing her Vulcan colleagues of the detention.

Most of them accepted it in proud, cold silence. Sefor, the senior Vulcan, served as spokesman for all of them when he demanded to know why they had to be detained in cells.

"As long as we are suspects, we will be watched and guarded. None of us can possibly escape the ship. Must we also suffer the humiliation of being locked up?"

T'Pris lowered her eyes, understanding the pride that made him ask the question, and she was ashamed at what she had to say next. "Commander Orloff and Dr. Boyce will be administering a truth-detector test to each of you while you are in the cells."

"A truth detector used on *Vulcans?* This is an insult, Lieutenant."

"I agree. But they have the right to apply it. A murder has been committed, and the Glory has been stolen. Someone must be lying."

"Someone, yes. But not necessarily a Vulcan."

"It is someone with the strength and the technique to commit the murder using *lan-dovna.* To your knowledge, could anyone other than a Vulcan do it?"

Sefor frowned deeply, his brows drawing together in a straight, dark line. Reluctantly, he sighed and said, "No. It seems to point only to a Vulcan, but I swear on my honor that I do not believe any one of our compatriots could or would commit such acts."

"The evidence does not agree."

"Evidence may be interpreted many ways, Lieutenant. With no hard clues, no witnesses, and no motive attributable to any one of us, it may be that the interpretation of the evidence is incorrect."

* * *

Boyce and Orloff stared at each other over the truth detector after the last Vulcan had completed the bout of questioning. The machine was sensitive not only to minute body responses—pulse, heart, degree of perspiration—but it had the capacity to register voice inflections that betrayed untruths as well.

"I don't believe it," Orloff grunted.

"I've never known this thing to fail," Boyce said.

The door of the interrogation room slid open, and the two men looked up as Number One entered. "Well, gentlemen?" She dropped gracefully into a chair opposite Boyce. The doctor looked away from her uncomfortably. "Am I jumping ahead too far if I guess the tests were inconclusive?"

"Not inconclusive," Boyce replied. "They were all negative."

"Excuse me?"

Boyce brought up the results on the detector's broad, flat screen. "According to this, they're *all* telling the truth."

"Could there be a malfunction?"

"It was tested before we began," Orloff said.

"We're talking about Vulcans. To a great extent, they control all emotions, even their voice levels—"

Orloff shook his head. "Boyce thought of that beforehand. We pre-tested on Lieutenant T'Pris. We asked her to throw in several lies to routine questions to check the machine's response to a Vulcan. It picked out the misstatements instantly."

"It's their sense of honor," Boyce put in. "To lie is dishonorable, shameful. Even for T'Pris, who only lied in order to check the machine's response, it was uncomfortable for her to do so—and the machine registered it."

"Difficult as it is to believe, Number One," Orloff said, "*this* evidence points to our suspects' being innocent."

"Then who in hell is guilty?" Number One looked at Boyce and Orloff in frustration. Neither man had an answer. The executive officer shook her head, stirring her long mane of dark hair around her shoulders. "No. Sorry. At least one of them *must* be lying—and able to hide it from the detector."

Once the sun dropped behind the mountains, darkness came swiftly to the Druncaras. Spock and Pike watched the village below. Lights began to glow in a number of windows, and the smell of cooking began to rise, wafted by a light breeze. As soon as it was dark enough to hide them from any casual watchers in the town, they began a slow and careful descent of the slope, angling toward the end of the village where the "prison" building stood a little apart from the others. The temperature had dropped as the sun had gone down, and the guard—a different one—had left his post beside the door to go inside. Though he couldn't see them, Pike knew Lieutenants Ars Dan and Endel were working their way down the flank of the hill at the other end of the village.

Pike's foot slipped on some loose pebbles, and the stones skittered and bounced down the slope. He and Spock froze where they were, scarcely breathing. There was no shout of discovery or any particular stir in the village. Something that sounded almost like a dog *wuffed* in a throaty bark, but it subsided after a moment. Normal night sounds continued—the flutter of a nocturnal hunting bird's wings overhead, the *shush* of the wind in the trees, some softly peeping insects in the long grass.

Spock and Pike moved ahead again, stepping carefully. They reached the bottom of the slope and gratefully dropped behind the cover of a woodpile that rose more than six feet in height. The cords of wood were stacked against the windowless side wall of the suspected prison building. The hours they had spent in observation had revealed that there was a back door to the building. No one seemed to use it, and it was probably locked. With the guard inside, the front entrance also was likely to be locked or barred. Much as he hated to do so, Pike had been forced to request phasers beamed down for himself and Spock. He hoped they would only have to use them to get into the building, and not in the sight of the mutants. The guards they had seen had not appeared to be armed, but small weapons could easily have been concealed in the bulky clothes they wore. Pike reached into the pocket of his desert robe and brought out his communicator. He flipped it open, muffling the characteristic beeping signal against his chest, then he spoke quietly.

"Pike to Endel."

"Here, sir," the throaty voice of the reptilian lieutenant whispered back from the communicator.

"Ready any time you are, Lieutenant."

"Aye, sir. Endel out."

Pike tucked away the communicator and pulled out the phaser pistol. Spock already had his ready. "Set it for cutting," Pike said softly. Spock nodded and quickly made the adjustment.

On the far side of the village, there was a sudden hollow *whump,* and a flash of light tore the night apart. The smell of smoke and the roar of flames rose immediately. Doors flew open, and the pounding of feet and alarmed shouts signaled that the mutants were leaping to the source of the disturbance. The hoarse *wuffing* of several dog-animals joined the din, the body of noise swiftly moving toward the opposite end of the town.

"Now," Pike snapped.

He and Spock leaped toward the rear door of the prison building. Taking positions on either side of the door, they aimed their phasers at the knob area and cut a shimmering line around it, the phaser beams slicing through the heavy wood like a hot knife through butter. Pike kicked the door in and entered first, Spock following close on his heels.

The interior of the small room was dark, cluttered with boxes and sacks, possibly a food storage area. Light gleamed around the edges of a door in the wall opposite them, and they moved toward it with military precision.

Suddenly, the door slammed open, and the mutant guard loomed in the entrance. Behind him, they could see the figures of a handsome boy and a lovely young girl, the boy arrested in the act of putting his arm protectively around the girl. The guard dodged aside, evading Spock's attempt to reach out and apply a Vulcan neck pinch. The mutant's arm slashed out, and the blow knocked the Vulcan back against the wall.

Pike sidestepped the guard's headlong lunge at him, tripped the mutant, and sent him sprawling. He lay still, stunned, and the two officers sprang into the main room.

Pike reached the girl as she seemed to cringe away from Bardan, and he pulled her up by the arm. Spock turned toward the boy, holding out a hand to assist him. Silene twisted as she was pulled toward Pike. Her *dree* knife flashed in her fist, and the viciously sharp blade sliced a long cut in Pike's robes, uncomfortably close to his ribs. Spock moved to try to pull Silene away from Pike. Bardan let out a roar of anger and flung himself at Spock, tackling the tall Vulcan and bringing him crashing to the floor. Pike found himself trying to hold a wildcat in check—a cursing, wriggling desert woman who was actively trying to cut out his heart.

Chapter Eleven

SPOCK HAD RECOVERED from his surprise at being
slammed to the ground by Bardan and pushed the boy
away from him to scramble to his feet. The boy clawed
up Spock's legs and managed to swing a punch that
Spock blocked. The Vulcan caught Bardan's arm and
twisted it behind him. There was a bloodcurdling roar
from the back room, and the mutant guard barreled
through the open door. Spock released Bardan, pushing the boy into the path of the mutant so that they
collided with a dull thump as he desperately struggled
to get his phaser reset on stun.

Pike had his hands full trying to subdue Silene, who
didn't seem to appreciate the fact that he was there to
rescue her. The girl expertly feinted with the knife
toward Pike's throat and then came in under his
guard, going for his midsection. He got an arm down
in time to block the thrust and divert it enough to
escape with only another harmless cut through the
robe, the sleeve this time. "Stop it!" he panted. "We're

trying to—" Silene slashed again. Pike finally managed to grab both her wrists so she couldn't work the knife. She promptly bit his arm.

The mutant guard pushed Bardan aside and leaped at Spock. Spock abandoned the phaser and side-stepped, pushing hard as the man rocketed past him to land in a heap, the breath knocked out of him. Bardan came at Spock again, but Spock fended him off with one hand long enough to reach down and deliver a Vulcan neck pinch to the guard. The mutant stiffened as the pressure point in his neck flamed, and then he slumped to the ground. Bardan broke away from Spock and lunged for his throat. Spock trapped the boy in a bear hug and lifted him, struggling, from the floor.

Pike wrenched his arm away from Silene's wicked teeth, spun her around, and finally trapped her arms behind her back. She tried to kick him, and he gave her a violent shake. "I said, *stop it!* We're here to rescue you."

"Go away!" Silene shouted. "We have no need of you!"

"What?" Pike stammered. He pulled Silene around to face him. "What did you say?"

"We're not going with you," Bardan snapped. He had stopped struggling, and Spock slowly released him. The boy and the girl stood glaring angrily at their would-be rescuers. "Let us alone."

"Your fathers want you back safe," Spock said.

"No. Our fathers want us back *apart.*" Silene moved over to the fallen mutant, who was starting to stir. Spock stared in astonishment. No one had ever shaken off a Vulcan neck pinch so quickly. As Silene helped the mutant to sit up, she said, "We are safe here."

Pike looked from one to the other in confusion. "But you were kidnapped by force, carried off, held prisoner here . . ."

"We were carried off by the mutants," Bardan agreed, "but we're not prisoners."

The mutant pushed to his feet, Silene hovering beside him. "Are you unharmed, Panlow?" she asked in concern.

He patted her arm reassuringly, squared himself around to face Pike and Spock. "I am Panlow, chief of this village. Who are you?"

"They were sent by our fathers."

There was a scuffling sound outside the door, and then it abruptly opened. An embarrassed Endel and Ars Dan were thrust unceremoniously into the room by several angry mutants. "They destroyed almost a cold turn's worth of firewood, Panlow," one of them grumbled angrily.

Ars Dan looked at Pike in chagrin and shrugged his shoulders. "Their dogs—I think they were dogs—hunted us down, sir. We were unable to escape them."

Panlow had been studying Spock, Endel, and Ars Dan with sharp interest. He moved toward them almost accusingly. "You are mutants like us, yet you wear the clothes of the desert, and you come here on the orders of the flatlanders. Why have you deserted your own kind?"

Spock shot a look at Pike, in that one glance requesting permission to speak for them. Pike nodded. "We are not of your kind, Panlow. We have learned to work in harmony with the flatlanders. We are not considered to be different in the way you are."

"There. You see?" Panlow cried to the other mutants who had crowded into the room. "There is hope for my plan. This is the proof of it. We need not be isolated in these mountains any longer. We can find a way to live with the others to the benefit of all."

Pike cleared his throat. "You still haven't explained about the abduction of these two."

"They've treated us with kindness," Bardan said. "They want us to be emissaries for them."

"Panlow?"

The mutant leader was almost unbelievably ugly, his face twisted into a grotesque parody of what was considered normal. His voice, however, had the timbre and quality of a trained speaker. Despite his ungainly body, when he moved there was a certain nobility and grace about him. He swept his four-fingered hand toward Silene and Bardan, and a smile warped his face. "I have planned for a long time to take some normals from the flatland, but they had to be young enough to accept us as we are. They also had to be old enough to understand that we wished to make contact with their people and why. These two, they fell into our hands as we moved closer to their lands to scout."

"They have much to offer our people," Silene said. "Things we have never been able to find or make for ourselves."

"That's true," Bardan put in. "They mine ores we've never even seen . . ."

"We control these mountains." Panlow nodded.

"And the ores and minerals that are rich here. We have the forests, the animals, birds, and fish that the flatlanders would find rare and exotic. There is wealth and abundance here that they can never have because they fear to venture into our territory. We have unique trade goods which would benefit them, and they have trade goods we need."

"I see," Pike said quietly. "What you really want is a chance to trade with the nomads and townspeople of the flatlands so all would benefit."

"Exactly." Panlow smiled. "We have spied on them when they have not known it. They are progressing, leaving the holocaust behind them. We wish to do so as well. These two children could be our bridge to understanding with the others of this planet."

Pike turned to Silene and Bardan. "What about you two? What do you think about all this?"

"When they carried us off, we were frightened," Silene said. "But they treated us with gentleness, with concern, as though they feared to hurt us. When we got past our terror, we saw them as people, not mutants."

"They believe we can help them, and I think we can. But we have to be able to talk to our people, especially our parents, as adults. I mean, *they* have to accept *us* as adults."

"You did run away against their wishes, instead of presenting your love to them as grownups."

Silene flared again, pushing toward Pike angrily. "They only saw us as spoiled children defying their wishes. They took no time to see us as two people who love each other."

Pike tilted his head and smiled charmingly at her.

"I'll grant you have a point there. I think it's only because you're both so very young. But I believe we might be able to assist you—and Panlow's people—to get what you want."

Orloff reported to Number One every half-hour, but it was clear both he and she were frustrated. Number One and T'Pris stayed on duty on the bridge while the majority of the security and engineering personnel searched the *Enterprise* rivet by rivet. After Orloff had reported one more time that nothing had been found, Number One irritably clicked off the intercom and looked at the Vulcan woman. "I feel like I'm chasing some kind of will-o'-the-wisp."

"I am not sure I understand the reference," T'Pris said politely.

"It means pursuing a goal that's not really there, an illusion. I believe the Glory is on this ship and we can find it. But I'm not sure we're going about it the right way. I think there's something I'm missing, but I don't know what it is." She smiled, and the smile softened the lines of her face into friendliness. "And if that sounds confused and frustrated, that's about right."

"Is it possible we are looking for two persons?" T'Pris asked. "It could be one was the murderer and one is an accomplice—possibly a non-Vulcan—who might move the Glory ahead of our search teams."

"Would a Vulcan murderer trust a non-Vulcan to do that with the Glory?"

T'Pris considered it, then shook her head. "The point is taken. I do not believe that would happen—*if* the murderer is a Vulcan."

"Are you back to that? I thought we'd all agreed only a Vulcan could have committed the murder in the way it was done."

"I believe humans have a saying, 'Never assume.' It appears to me we have all been guilty of assuming only a Vulcan could or would use the *lan-dovna* technique to murder Meadows. I admit it seems so obvious, but perhaps that is what the killer meant us to assume. Our traditions and rituals are not secret on this subject. As Spock pointed out to you, it is a self-defense technique that is taught. There are many who have studied our philosophy and combat techniques, though it is seldom that a non-Vulcan has the strength to carry out many of them. Still, if we allow for the strength, a non-Vulcan could very possibly execute *lan-dovna*. I wish to follow a theory that our criminal is not a Vulcan. If we take that assumption, what other candidates on board do we have?"

Number One thought about it, liked the possibilities, and nodded to T'Pris. "All right, Lieutenant. Follow that line of thought and bring the answers back to me. Who else might have committed this murder, and why?"

"C'mon, Scotty," Bob Brien hissed. "They're right behind us."

Scott moved a little faster down the corridor, walking with a peculiarly stiff-legged gait. Brien, carrying an inconspicuous toolbox, hurried on ahead. He stopped again and impatiently waved Scott on. Scott angrily hobbled up to him. "It isn't easy to run with three distillery pipes down your pants leg!" He gestured at Brien's toolbox. "You get to carry all the small parts and catch jars in there."

"Well, it was *your* idea to transport them that way. Come on, now." Brien nervously threw a look down the corridor behind them. "Security's through with the engineering search. We can circle around and go back in through the number four entry. There's a service closet there—it has to have been inspected already. We'll dump all these parts in there until you go back on shift tonight."

"About time, too. I may never be able to walk right again." Scott awkwardly hitched his left leg along, unable to flex his knee.

Brien tipped him his twinkle-eyed grin and patted his shoulder. "It's worth it. I delivered all the jars we had in stock, and there's a whole batch of orders to fill when you get set up again."

"Bob, I'm starting to believe you're money mad. Do ye see yourself as a tycoon or some such?"

"Tycoon? We're just above breaking even on this. No, it's the happy, smiling faces I see when our crewmates take a taste of this first-class hooch you've concocted. And a happy crew is—a happy crew."

Scott grunted as they finally reached the engineering entry. "Agreed. But just above breaking even—" He paused thoughtfully. "We should have a better profit margin."

Phil Boyce finished the last of his sick-call chores— no more heavy than usual. There were the usual small accidents people suffered—bruises and cuts, a head cold (that common ailment still had no sure cure), an upset stomach from overindulgence in a particularly rich dessert the night before. Boyce cleared away his instruments and left sickbay in the charge of his head nurse.

He stopped in the rec room for a cup of coffee. *Must be the atmosphere or something,* Boyce thought. Rec-room coffee always tasted better than sickbay coffee, even though it was actually piped from the same source before being delivered through the food slots. As he sat at a table sipping the brew and casually glancing around at the other off-duty personnel in the room, Boyce noticed a common phenomenon and realized he had actually been seeing it for several days. He tossed down the rest of his coffee and went to a nearby wall intercom.

"Dr. Boyce calling Number One."

Her voice came on instantly. *"Number One here."*

"Where are you?"

"Bridge."

"I'm coming up."

When the lift doors swished aside for him, Number One turned to look at him from the command chair. "Something wrong?"

"Just something odd." He moved to her side and stood there, thinking about it. Her restless little move in the chair brought his attention back from his musings. "Sorry. I realized I've been seeing it the past couple of days and not paying much attention to it," he said abruptly. "Have you noticed that a lot of our crew members seem to be smiling a lot lately?"

"Phil . . ." she said dangerously. The warning was implicit in the tone of her voice: *Don't waste my time.*

"Oh, I don't mean *just* happy. The ones I'm talking about have this fatuous little half-smile on their faces, and their eyes look kind of glazed."

"Are you suggesting this crew is bazorged? Smashed? Looped? Three sheets to the wind? *Drunk?*"

"Well, not on duty. It's the off-duty ones I'm seeing."

"You're sure?"

"They have all the signs of being sloshed to the gills."

She thought it over, then nodded briskly. "All right. Haul in everyone who's suspect and check them over. Off duty is one thing, but if anyone came on duty in that condition, it could present a danger to ship operations."

"I suspect it's that new hooch. Inside gossip says it's all over the ship."

"Source?"

"For the hooch? Nobody's talking on that one. The stuff's too good."

Number One sniffed and shook her head. "It's no good if it affects the crew like this. Get on those exams, Phil. It's important we find out exactly what's happening."

T'Pris had been excused from other duties to concentrate on her investigation into other possible suspects. She had opted to tap into the library computer from her station in the biology lab, and she had been busy at it for hours.

When she came off duty on the bridge at four o'clock, Number One decided to see if T'Pris had made any progress. As she entered the biology lab, T'Pris was taking a brief break from the computer, rubbing eyes that were tired from staring continuously at the screen.

Number One smiled at her encouragingly. "You don't have to spend every minute on this, Lieutenant. Take an hour break and relax."

"No, I cannot. It is important to our honor that I discover who else other than a Vulcan might have committed this murder."

"Have it your way, then. Have you found anything, any leads at all?"

"I ordered up detailed personnel records on every crew member. Not just the service jackets—personal history. The kind of thing Starfleet has in depth on every member of the fleet."

Number One raised an eyebrow. "That information is strictly classified."

"Yes, but we are discussing a murder here. On Commander Orloff's request, Starfleet has opened the records of personnel on this ship to me. I believe I might have found an interesting line of information to pursue. Something promising, but I do not have it all yet."

"Notify me when you do."

"As soon as I can verify all the data."

Number One nodded to her and left the lab. T'Pris hurried back to her station and renewed her pursuit of one little thread of information she had discovered, one that promised a revelation if her assumption was correct.

* * *

Phil Boyce was studying one more overhead diagnostic screen as the patient in hand lay on the sickbay bed smiling vacuously and staring into space. He sighed and ran his instruments over the body one more time; they confirmed what the overhead was telling him.

"All right, you can get up," he said. The crewman remained prone, smiling. Boyce gestured to the assisting nurse. "Give him a hand, Nurse Blayton." He turned away to find Number One waiting for him at the sickbay door. He jerked a nod toward his office. "Come on in."

The exec slumped down in a seat across from Boyce and waited. Boyce sat down and shook his head. "Never saw anything like it."

"Like what?"

"Technically, they're all drunk as skunks. Alcohol content in their blood is sky high. There's some disorientation, a certain loss of motor and speech reflexes, but no physical discomfort. There is one little thing that bothers me because I can't figure it out."

"It's the little things that kill you, Phil. What is it?"

"They all admit to consuming engine-room hooch, but every one of them swears he had no more than two drinks. Of course, they don't seem to remember much after that, but one or two drinks shouldn't have this effect on people—not all of them, anyway."

"You and I each had a glass of that hooch not too long ago. I wasn't affected. Were you?"

"No, but then the symptoms indicate we might not remember whether or not we *were* affected." Number One threw him a warning look, and he amended his statement. "I know I wasn't. I had minor surgery to perform that afternoon, and Blayton confirms my memory that I was functioning normally. But remember, you and I only had a half-shot apiece, not full glasses of the stuff." Boyce tapped his fingers on the desk, running it through his mind again. "All I can think of is some kind of contamination. I've never seen anything like it. Usually the stuff is potent but no more harmful than a double shot of Saurian brandy. This is something different."

Number One sighed and shifted her weight in the chair. "So it seems as though another search is in order, this time for a contaminated still."

"Couldn't you just order the culprit to come forward in the interests of public health?"

"You know damn well the making of engine-room hooch usually has a blind eye turned on it, but it's still illegal. The bootlegger can face a stiff demerit penalty, possibly loss of a commission. You don't think the contamination is deliberate, do you?"

"No, I don't. This effect is so unusual, I don't think anyone could've planned it."

"So, a mistake. I don't believe in penalizing an honest mistake if I don't have to. We'll have to find the still, though, and disable it, and then broadcast the reason for our action."

"What about the search for the Glory?"

Number One somberly shook her head. "No sign of it. This ship has been swept, dusted, and polished inside and out looking for it—and *nothing.*"

"It has to be here."

"I agree, unless someone destroyed it—and I can't

imagine why anyone would do that, not after killing for it."

Now she had it. T'Pris was elated. Here was the trail that led to the answer. It was a matter of logic, once one saw all the facts laid out. It was late; she had not taken a break to eat or rest for hours, but the exhilaration of the hunt gave her the adrenaline surge she needed to keep going. Her attention was so deeply rooted in the puzzle she had been slowly unraveling that her reflexes were just a fraction slow. She didn't realize someone was behind her until the very last moment. Then she heard the soft scrape of a boot sole on the hard deck.

The pungent smoke of cookfires rose over the *kerra* trees of Tisirah Oasis as the women prepared supper for the men in the dusk. It had been five days since Silene and Bardan had disappeared, four since the man known as Krees had gone looking for them with his mutant aides. Melkor Aliat had sent word back to his household and his shop that he would not return until Bardan's fate had been determined. A number of the townsmen who had accompanied Aliat this far had returned to Sendai, but several friends remained with him. They would have pitched a lonely camp under the trees with only bedrolls and a borrowed cookpot had not Ingarin insisted on having them join her family for meals. With that courtesy extended to strangers, *Shinsei* Farnah could not avoid inviting them to sleep under cover of the family tent.

After an initial wariness, the two fathers found a

number of subjects to discuss—and a number of
common opinions they shared, especially in regard to
trade. Both men sadly had come to the conclusion
that their children were lost to them forever. If
Indallah Krees and his strange assistants returned, the
fathers were convinced it would be with the bodies of
their son and daughter. Ingarin and *Makleh* Berendel
kept their own counsels and with far more faith than
the men.

Ingarin was presiding over her daughters-in-law as
they prepared the evening meal, when she suddenly
straightened, alert and listening. "What is it, Mother?" one of the young women asked, but Ingarin
shushed her. Gradually, it could be heard, far off but
distinct. The wind carried the soft tinkle of many
small bells, all jingling in a gentle rhythm.

"Someone comes from the Druncaras!" The cry
came from a lookout posted high in a *kerra* tree. The
entire camp surged as one to the edge of the oasis to
see who it was.

They came along the trail from the Druncara Range
slowly. The pack animals were so heavily laden that
they could move no faster than an ambling walk
which sounded the cheerful bells attached to their
harnesses. No less than thirty animals made up the
caravan, each watched over and chivied along by a
brawny mutant. Pike, Spock, Endel, and Ars Dan rode
the *meercans* borrowed from Farnah, pacing sedately
at the side of the caravan. Silene and Bardan led the
party mounted on *meercans* richly caparisoned with
beautifully woven exotic cloth of bold colors laced
with metallic thread.

Farnah stared along the road, shading his eyes with one hand. "It's them! They're alive!" he cried. He clapped Melkor Aliat on the shoulder. "It *is* them!" He scowled suddenly as he looked a little closer at the approaching animals. "On my two best *meercans* . . ."

Silene and Bardan led the caravan into the oasis. Pike had thought there would be cheering, but the nomads and the few townspeople among them were quiet, warily drawing back away from the mutants. If the mutants were aware of it, they gave no sign, merely prodding the pack animals along with intricately carved walking sticks. The two young people stopped near the tents and dismounted, tossing the reins of their mounts down in a ground hitch. The pack animals halted behind them, Pike and the others sliding off their mounts and moving after Silene and Bardan.

Silene reached out toward Bardan, and they approached their fathers hand in hand. Ingarin sized up Bardan with a nod of satisfaction. The boy had some strength to him, or her daughter would not have chosen him. He was a good-looking lad, and Silene seemed to be deferring to him, something she would never do if she did not respect him.

"Father . . ." Bardan began.

Aliat and Farnah moved forward at the same time, reaching out to enfold their children in their arms. "You're well? You're unharmed?"

"Yes, yes," Silene assured Farnah. "We were well treated."

"You young whelp, you've caused us a great deal of

worry." Aliat shook his son's shoulder, dropping into irritation now that the danger was over. "Bad enough you ran off without any consideration for me or our business. But to run off for this girl—"

"She ran off for *me.*"

"The more fools the both of you, then," Farnah snapped. He grabbed Silene's hand and started to pull her away toward the main tent. "Come then, Silene, back where you belong."

Silene dug in her heels and yanked hard, breaking free of her father's grip. "No!"

"Daughter—"

"Shinsei Farnah, I suggest you address the new mutant ambassadors in a more respectful manner," Pike said quietly but pointedly.

Farnah and Aliat turned toward him, both staring in astonishment. "What?" Farnah stammered. "What?"

"What do you mean, mutant ambassadors?" Aliat demanded.

"I mean exactly what I said, Trader Aliat. Panlow, the mutant leader, has adopted Bardan and Silene as his children."

"What!" Farnah roared.

Pike ignored the angry bellow and went on. "And he has given them the power to speak for him among you, to trade with you."

"Trade with the mutants?" Aliat snorted in derision. "What could they possibly have to trade that we might want?"

"They've brought a few offerings with them which you might care to examine." Pike winked at Silene.

The girl gestured to the mutants beside the pack animals. They immediately began to unload the packs, spreading ground cloths on which to lay out the merchandise for inspection. The nomads and the townsmen gathered closer in curiosity. Pike had to admit Panlow's men played their parts well, bringing out the different items one by one and then adding to each pile, every piece different and more intricate than the previous.

The onlookers began to whisper, to nudge each other. Silene and Bardan moved among the mutants, picking up and displaying items so that they could be better seen. There were glittering gemstones, some rough and some faceted, some of them set in intricately wrought gold and silver jewelry; luxuriously thick furs, several made into hoods and capes; richly colored and glazed dishes, jars, goblets, and pots. A gasp went up among the nomads when a mutant laid out a small armory of steel-bladed knives, swords, and lances.

Bardan smiled and took a jug from one of several set out on a ground cloth. He uncapped the jug, caught up two of the pottery goblets, and poured a ruby liquid into each. He graciously offered the goblets to his father and Farnah.

"The wines of the highlands are especially fine," he said smoothly. "The soil and the weather there are all particularly conducive to the cultivation of grapes."

The two older men sipped hesitantly at first and then appreciatively. Farnah stared into the goblet, rolling the sip of wine around his mouth and then swallowing. "It is rich and full-bodied," he commented to Aliat. "Not sour and thin like your wines."

Aliat scowled at the critical remark. "Not harsh enough to remove paint and tan *ucha* hide like yours, either," he shot back. He turned to Bardan. "We can offer ten *keshels* for each gallon jar of this wine."

Bardan's eyebrows rose. "Father, there is no need to be insulting. The mutants are prepared to *trade,* not to give their goods away."

"It was a fair offer!"

"Not for wine of this quality, which no one else has."

"We offer fifteen *keshels* for each gallon jar," Farnah suddenly said.

"We could be the exclusive dealers in Sendai, Bardan," Aliat insisted. "Surely the sole distributor should get a discount."

"Perhaps," Bardan agreed. "But our clients—that is, our people—have no desire to have any exclusive distributors dispensing their merchandise. They will deal fairly with all who wish to trade."

"Twenty *keshels* for each?" Farnah put in.

Bardan smiled at him. "Silene's father is as wise a man and as clever a trader as she has told me. Twenty *keshels* a jar is a good price. How many will you want, Shinsei Farnah?"

"A moment, my son. I, too, wish to place an order," Aliat said.

"At twenty *keshels* a jar, of course," Bardan replied firmly. "I cannot possibly take less."

"Oh, very well. Twenty a jar."

"Done." Bardan smiled. He brought out a bead counter and a writing sheet to keep track of the orders and the prices. "I would also like to have you sample the crystal wine, an outstanding white wine I believe you will enjoy . . ."

Pike, Spock, Endel, and Ars Dan stood quietly aside, watching the progress of the trading. Everyone was openly interested in the items on display. The women were particularly taken with the furs and silken cloth Silene was busily showing them. She called up her mother and Berendel and draped them both in yards of fine material to demonstrate how well the colors looked, how softly the cloth fell.

"You know, Spock, I have a feeling those two kids are going to handle their new responsibilities pretty well."

"I agree, sir. They are not quite the same children who ran away to defy their parents and please themselves," Spock said quietly. "They have made choices that have placed them here. They chose to run away to make their own lives. They chose to trust the mutants who carried them off. They chose to accept the role of ambassadors and negotiators between the mutants and their own people—a good indication they were ready to take on an adult role in their lives."

Pike studied the trading scene before him. The nomads had started to bring out some of their trade goods. Aliat and his townsmen begged for time to return to Sendai and bring back merchandise of their own. Silene and several mutants were marking off spaces where booths could be set up around the oasis pool.

Bardan climbed up on a large rock at poolside and called for quiet. "There is a great deal of bartering to be done here. You all have merchandise to sell and trade. We have begun to lay out booth spaces, enough for all. In four days' time we will conduct a trade fair here. Anyone with goods to sell will be welcome. But tonight, we will celebrate the bonding ceremony of Silene to me and me to her!"

There was a cheer of approval from most of the onlookers, including Ingarin and Berendel, Pike noticed. *Shinsei* Farnah and Melkor Aliat were not quite as happy as everyone else, but they would have to make the best of it. Their children were determined to work out their own future.

"I don't think we should allow ourselves the luxury of staying for the wedding, Spock. These people are well on their way to building an integrated society by themselves, and I think we should leave them to it."

"Will they not notice our disappearance, Captain?"

"They know I'm a wanderer, Spock, and the rest of you are mutants. No one will really question our slipping away."

Spock nodded, his eyes on the happy couple in the middle of a group of well-wishers. That should be the way he and T'Pris celebrated their togetherness. He was formally bound to T'Pring, but there were ways to end the betrothal, even now. They were frowned upon, but they were legally acceptable. Sarek would be furious, Amanda would be disappointed, but Spock would finally feel satisfied in himself. He had felt uneasy about T'Pring for a long time—her coldness and her distance made him uncomfortable with her. He knew he had never loved her; he had desired to please her to honor his obligation. It was only their parents who had chosen to try to join them. T'Pris was the woman who owned his heart. T'Pring would never be more than someone who had been assigned to marry him. If they married, she would keep up the appearances expected of her—but only on Vulcan. T'Pris would be with him, united in their careers as well as in marriage. It was better ended between him and T'Pring, and the sooner the better.

Pike touched Spock's arm, jerked his head toward the trees at the edge of the oasis. The other two lieutenants followed them as they drifted away from the busy group of traders still hovering around the displayed merchandise. Quietly, unnoticed, the four officers reached the far side of the grove. When they were safely screened by the trees, Pike brought out his communicator and flipped it open. "Pike to *Enterprise.*"

"Enterprise *here,*" came the immediate response.

"Four to beam up."

"Aye, sir."

There was a moment's wait as the order was relayed down to the transporter room. Then the familiar hum began to sing in the air, and the men froze as the atmosphere around them began to sparkle. The glittering transporter beam covered them completely as the hum rose to a whine, and then they were gone.

Number One was waiting for them in Transporter Room 3 when they beamed in. As soon as transportation was complete and the men moved off the platform, the executive officer stepped forward. Pike knew from her face that there was more trouble.

"Number One?"

"I'm sorry, sir. There's been another murder on board—the same method as the first." She looked pityingly at Spock. "The victim was Lieutenant T'Pris."

Chapter Twelve

SPOCK'S FACE WAS IMMOBILE; although he wanted to cry, he refused to let the tears form. His body trembled violently. "Where is T'Pris?" he demanded hoarsely.

"Her body was removed to sickbay," Number One said kindly.

Both Pike and the exec were watching him closely. Spock didn't care. He moved toward the transporter-room door, weaving uncertainly, staggered by his grief. "I must see her."

"Dr. Boyce will show you where she is."

"Alone," Spock snapped. The doors slid open before him.

"Call Boyce and tell him," Pike ordered quietly. Number One moved to the intercom on the transporter console as Spock exited and the doors swished closed.

T'Pris's body had been removed from the lab where she had been found and placed in a private alcove of sickbay. Boyce had folded her hands over her breast and closed her eyes. When Spock saw her, it was easy to think for a moment that she was merely asleep. The illusion lasted only until Spock reached out to touch her lovely face and felt the coldness of her flesh.

The doctor had retreated to his office when Spock entered, shutting the door behind him. Spock dimly realized he was alone and was grateful no one heard the chest-wrenching sobs that broke from him as he bent over T'Pris's body. He took her hand in his and held it while he leaned down to kiss her one last time. A teardrop fell and dampened her gentle face. Spock released her hand and straightened his shoulders. He had to use his sleeve to wipe away his tears, and as he did so his face changed.

Hardened.

A cold rage and desire for revenge rose in Spock. The woman he had loved was dead, and her murderer had also killed Spock's hope that he might find happiness. He felt he would never know another woman to whom he could give himself so completely.

Later in his quarters, Spock sat motionless before the ancestral figure from his family shrine. He should have been meditating, but he found his grief was too great for his mind to focus on a mantra or the riddle of a Vulcan *koan*. The only image that filled his mind was T'Pris—alive, smiling at him, her face and body flushed with lovemaking, full of the deep and unspeakable joy of mental and physical bonding that only Vulcans could feel.

Meditation should have brought him peace, but the anger and need for revenge would not release its hold on him. Finally, he gave it up, pushed to his feet, and went to seek out the captain.

Pike sat with Number One in the briefing room, going over what they knew, which the executive officer had to admit was not much. "She was murdered in exactly the same way as Meadows," Number One said. "With the right hand and with what the Vulcans call *lan-dovna* technique—one-handed strangulation."

"The Vulcans on board?" Pike asked quickly.

"All of them were under house arrest, observed to be in their quarters at the time, sir."

"Then who in hell could possibly have done it?"

The door slid open, and Spock entered. "I beg pardon for the intrusion, Captain."

"You've been relieved from duty for the time being, Spock," Pike said. He glanced across the table at Number One, recalling what she had told him about Spock and T'Pris's personal involvement.

"Again, I beg pardon, sir, but I believe I would be more valuable to you in the investigation of these murders if I were *on* duty. In fact, it is my belief that I should have been pursuing the investigation all along, and Lieutenant T'Pris should have gone to the planet surface to assist you there."

He blames himself for her death, Pike thought. *And I'm not going to let him get away with that.* "No, Mr. Spock. I needed you there, and the lieutenant was perfectly suited to the task here. No one could have known the murderer was not one of the suspects we had in hand."

"I would not have been such easy prey," Spock said harshly. "Captain, I wish to continue this investigation with you."

214

"I see no reason why Lieutenant Spock's request should not be granted, sir," Number One put in.

Pike traded a long look with his executive officer. They both knew this would mean a great deal to Spock. If he was blaming himself for putting T'Pris in line of danger, assisting in the search for her murderer would be an expiation for that guilt. "I agree." Pike gestured to a seat next to the first officer. "Number One was just filling in the details for me."

Quickly, Number One outlined the steps that had been taken to discover the murderer and the fact that truth detectors had failed to uncover any lie in the Vulcans' stories of innocence. "T'Pris noticed that Meadows's computer had no files or notes of any kind on the Glory, and he most certainly would have made some. She thought the murderer had erased any information Meadows had recorded. We found the same situation in T'Pris's library-computer link after her death. She had been pursuing a line of information she had found in the personnel files. She thought the most viable suspect—if Vulcans were in the clear—would be someone at least familiar with Vulcan and its martial defense arts. I saw her working at her computer link. I know she was making notes. When we found her body, I checked the computer myself. Any files or records she had made were gone, erased."

Spock eagerly leaned toward her. "Tell me what she said, any reference at all to her line of investigation, her reasoning. Can you recall it, Number One?"

"Of course." Number One looked slightly miffed. She had an eidetic memory. "We spoke of possible suspects, and T'Pris said, 'I believe humans have a saying, "Never assume." It appears to me we have all been guilty of assuming only a Vulcan could or would use the *lan-dovna* technique to murder Meadows. I admit it seems so obvious, but perhaps that is what the killer meant us to assume. Our traditions and rituals are not secret on this subject. As Spock pointed out to you, it is a self-defense technique that is taught. There are many who have studied our philosophy and combat techniques, though it is seldom that a non-Vulcan has the strength to carry out many of them. Still, if we allow for the strength, a non-Vulcan could very possibly execute *lan-dovna*. I wish to follow a theory that our criminal is not a Vulcan. If we take that assumption, what other candidates on board do we have?' Then, when she was following up on the library-computer link, she said, 'I ordered up detailed personnel records on every crew member. Not just the service jackets—personal history. The kind of thing Starfleet has in depth on every member of the fleet.' It was in those records that she seemed to have found something that was leading her somewhere. She said it was 'something promising,' but she didn't have all the facts yet. I believe she was following that trail when she was murdered, and the murderer erased all information she had compiled."

When she finished, Spock nodded thoughtfully. "I see." He paused a moment, then looked at the captain. "May I see where T'Pris died?"

Orloff had sealed off the biology lab, but Pike broke the seals without hesitation and allowed Spock to precede him into the room. It was a small but efficient office adjoining the larger lab area where specimens were examined and scanned. The computer screen still glowed, but it showed only a dull, blank face to them as they examined it.

"Are any other files missing?" Pike asked Number One.

"None that we can determine. All routine duty reports by the science officer on duty were logged. The other lab technicians and biologists say there was little to do on this leg of the mission except pursue theoretical work. Some of T'Pris's research is in the computer. But her line of inquiry regarding personnel records is totally gone."

"Not totally, Number One."

Pike and Number One looked around at Spock as he seated himself at the computer console.

"Lieutenant, I assure you we ran a full scan of all records in the library computer, and T'Pris's are not there, except for the biological research in which she had been engaged."

"I agree they have been erased. But not as thoroughly as our murderer would like to have had them."

"Explain," Pike said.

"I am an A-5 computer expert, Captain."

Pike smiled wryly, recalling Number One's briefing on Lieutenant Spock. *The best most officers attain is an A-3 rating,* Pike had observed. *Precisely, sir.* Number One had made her point with those two words. Their new Vulcan lieutenant had exceptional qualifications. It was unfortunate they would be called on to find his loved one's murderer. "Go on," Pike said.

"What most people, including Starfleet officers, do not fully appreciate is that any thorough investigative probe into computer records can reveal what may be referred to as footprints, even in the case of an erased record or one that apparently has been completely destroyed. The computer memory retains at least the ghost of an imprint of that record. Therefore, no file is ever totally lost. I need only to follow the trail of footprints to recreate the records T'Pris was investigating."

"How soon can that be done?"

"Ah," Spock sighed. "I did not mean to make the task appear easy. It is a process of reconstruction, of hunting out the faintest of signs and symbols among the many tracks available in the library computer. It will take a while, captain. I cannot speculate on the number of hours."

"Then I believe you should get started."

Spock nodded briskly. "Yes, sir." He turned to the library-computer link and began work without another look at the captain and Number One.

Scott had left the various pieces of the still in the engineering service closet for more than forty-eight hours. Brien was urging him to get the distillery in operation again, but Scott was wary of an unexpected sweep of the engineering section.

"We have customers to please, Scotty," Brien pleaded. "They won't wait forever."

"They'll have to, won't they?" Scott retorted stubbornly. "Won't do them a bit of good if security confiscates it all, will it? Do you know what they'll do if they find out who's the owner of that little piece of piping? They'll reduce me and you to ensigns all over again. They'll put us in charge of the engineering shift on a scow collecting the bits and pieces of space junk in Earth orbit. We'll get a leave maybe in twenty-five years, if we're lucky. No, man. Let it alone a while. There's no one will miss a jug or two, and as ye said yourself, this is a drop of the stuff worth waitin' for."

Caitlin Barry was conducting a routine inspection of the dilithium crystal in the central core. While they maintained standard orbit over Areta on impulse power, the warp engines were cut back to the minimum operating level, and it was a good time to run all the standard checks. It was midshift, and Bob Brien was assisting her as they ran through the routine.

She approached the inspection scope hole which would afford her a view of the underside of the crystal hanging in its cradle in the core. "Ready?" she asked over her shoulder.

Brien acknowledged he was, bringing up the clipboard he carried. Caitlin flipped open the inspection port and levered the close inspection lens in front of her eyes. The end of the lens which scoped the underside of the crystal had a series of mirrors built into it so that the maneuvering of a toggle enabled the viewer to see all areas of the crystal from this angle. Caitlin put her eye to the lens and worked the toggle slowly so that the system gave her a series of close-up views one after the other.

"Hold it," Caitlin said suddenly. She froze the lens where it was and magnified the image. "Got a crack."

"How bad?" Brien asked, stylus poised over the clipboard.

"Simple hairline fracture. Lucky we spotted it now, though. If it had gotten any bigger, it could have cracked in midwarp, rupturing the whole crystal." She looked back at him pointedly. There was no need to discuss what would happen if the crystal ruptured. The carefully aimed streams of matter and antimatter would have mingled directly without the controlling medium of the dilithium between, and the *Enterprise* would have been blown to space dust in microseconds. "All right, let's get it out of there."

The section on duty could handle it, although removal and replacement of a crystal wasn't simple. First, all warp functions had to be shut down. Then the damaged crystal had to be lifted out of its cradle using waldos manipulated by two people, carefully edged to the loading chute, eased into that, and dropped into the protective cartridge that would carry it away for disposal. The replacement crystal had to be lifted into the core, boosted slowly into the catching manipulators of the waldos, and then gently maneuvered into the main cradle. Once there, it would be precisely aligned and tested, and finally the warp engines could be run up again.

Caitlin supervised the shutdown of the engines and decided to allow the duty team to remove the crystal under Brien's supervision. She went to the observation scope to watch the removal. Opening the scope hole, she casually glanced along the length of it before applying her eye to the lens. There was a peculiar little mark on the side of the scope hole which she hadn't noticed before—circular and definitely out of place. Frowning, she slid the lens up and out of the way and reached in to run her fingers over the marred surface. Her nails caught on the far edge of the circle and lifted a flat lid, revealing the small hole cut into the metal.

"What in the world?"

Bob Brien was too busy supervising the crystal removal team to notice that the chief engineer had found something odd in the inspection scope hole. He didn't see her get a probe and run it down that mysterious opening. The probe end ran a little way and then reappeared, dangling among the irregular latticework of pipes that decorated the bulkhead about four feet away. Caitlin studied it thoughtfully. The still would have been beautifully camouflaged in the eye-deceiving tangle. When you knew where to look, it was easy to see where it had been, but she knew she had passed by without seeing it countless times.

Caitlin was no stranger to the existence of engine-room hooch. She was also aware of the fact that someone had been diligently brewing up batch after batch on this voyage—with some detriment to off-duty personnel, according to Boyce and Number One. She had not been able to figure out where the still had been located—until this moment. The thing must have been removed during the engine-room search for the Glory, but where was it now?

Caitlin retired to her small office off the main engineering section, put her feet up on her desk, and leaned back to think about it a while. No one had offered the chief a sample of the contraband alcohol—she seldom drank—but she had heard it had a dynamic quality. Number One and Dr. Boyce had informed her the day before that it was potentially dangerous. The engine-room searches had obviously cut off production, and the culprits were lying low for the moment. If she were making the hooch, she would want the equipment nearby so she could resume activity as soon as possible. She brought her boots down to the deck with an easy jackknife of her knees. A likely place had occurred to her.

She asked no one to accompany her. The duty crew was busy with the dilithium crystal replacement in any event. The first three service closets Caitlin investigated held no more than the expected tools and supplies. She mentally noted that the supply shelves were fully stocked and efficiently arranged. Good housekeeping, she thought approvingly. Service Closet 4 was different. It contained an additional several pipes, two of them curled and rippling and two short and straight—definitely nonstandard equipment— and a tool kit that should not have been there. Caitlin bent and flipped open the kit, revealing a neat arrangement of tools, pipe fittings, and two small catch jars. The tool kit had no identifying marks; it was standard Starfleet issue. Whose?

Spock rubbed his tired eyes, trying to ignore the burning sensation and the heaviness of his lids. He had been seated in front of the library-computer screen in the biology lab for almost twenty hours, and fatigue had begun to drag at him, dulling his mental perception.

T'Pris had been examining the complete personnel records of all crew members—the lives of two hundred three people, including family histories that traced three and even four generations. Many of the crew came from fleet families—service that dated back to the pioneer days of space exploration and the beginnings of Starfleet. Others had been drawn into the service by the romance and adventure promised by the drive to push back the known boundaries of space. The galaxy was so vast only a small percentage of it had been mapped and explored; the Milky Way was a treasure house of unknown worlds and civilizations. Some might prove friendly, some hostile, but all would be endlessly fascinating.

Spock was so distracted by weariness and the overwhelming volume of facts the library computer was sending that he almost missed the clue. He passed it by, registering it in his subconscious a moment before he realized what he had seen. He ran back to it. There. So small a fact to be so monumentally important, but as he looked at it again, Spock knew this was the answer.

Pike was shocked at Spock's appearance as the Vulcan entered the briefing room and stood swaying in fatigue before himself and Number One. His complexion was incredibly sallow, and huge black hollows resembling bruises smudged the area under his eyes.

"Captain," Spock said wearily. "I believe I know who the murderer is."

"Excellent, Mr. Spock."

"But I do not know the motive," Spock went on. "At least, the motive for Meadows's murder. I believe T'Pris was killed because she was on the track of the murderer's identity. The reasons for the initial crime are unclear to me."

"But who is it, Spock?"

Spock levelly met Pike's look and sidestepped the question. "Sir, I am about to make an unusual request. I hope you will grant it."

Pike glanced at Number One, frowning slightly. Spock was deliberately keeping the name from them. "Let's hear it."

"I want to draw the murderer out on my own. I want to elicit a confession and a motive, and I want every Vulcan on board to be able to hear it, too."

"Why?" Pike snapped.

"This was a Vulcan execution, not only in method but in one of the victims. A Vulcan committed the murders and stole the Glory."

Pike stared accusingly at his first officer. "You and Orloff swore all the Vulcans had proven their innocence."

"They did, sir, positively."

"Number One is correct, Captain," Spock interrupted quietly.

"Then what are you talking about?"

Spock's face hardened, his eyes angrily darkening into implacable coldness. "It would be more correct to say all *known* Vulcans were proven innocent. Do I have your permission to handle this murderer in my own way?"

Pike didn't like it. It smelled of personal vengeance, and it seemed totally unlike the Vulcan second officer who had reported aboard only two weeks ago. Pike had a feeling the old Spock would have been appalled at the suggestion of his being an instrument of revenge. The man who faced him now obviously had embraced the idea and was exceedingly willing to carry it out.

"I'm sorry, but I have to question your motives on this, Spock."

"They are personal, sir. My relationship with Lieutenant T'Pris was . . . close. More than that, one Vulcan has committed crimes that cast dishonor on all Vulcans, but particularly on those of this ship. I know the identity of the criminal, but that is not enough. I must know *why* the crimes were committed. This is a Vulcan matter, Captain. To let anyone else handle it would be . . . unacceptable."

"To you or the others?"

"To all Vulcan, sir."

Pike thought it over, not liking the idea of security not handling the capture, if Spock was right. Yet Spock had a point if the entire crime—the theft of the Glory and the two murders—did revolve around Vulcans. How the devil could the murderer be a Vulcan and not known to them? Still, however it was, Spock believed he had smelled out the killer and now wanted it to be a Vulcan capture. Given the high sense of Vulcan honor and Spock's personal involvement with T'Pris, Pike could sympathize with the request.

The captain finally nodded. "Orloff should be present."

"I will keep the commander informed. Indeed, I will require his assistance in one or two arrangements that need to be made. The culprit will be turned over to security when the time comes."

"Very well, Mr. Spock. Make your arrangements."

Caitlin Barry called together all the new engineering personnel after she made sure the dilithium crystal had been properly installed and all tests run to check its soundness and its alignment. The restarting of the warp engines was under way, and the entire system would be on line again in a matter of hours. The engineers stood in front of her at attention in a formal line.

"Ladies and gentlemen," she said as she moved down the line. "You're all aware of the existence of a still on this ship. You and I both know that while it's unusual, there are nonengineering officers who are capable of whipping up a batch of hooch but not many. You and I both know that one of *you* is the most likely moonshiner." No one looked at her; all eyes were kept straight ahead. Every face was expressionless. "They tell me the supply that's been coming out of this particular still has been of an unusually interesting and intoxicating nature. Dr. Boyce and I have discovered there's a reason for that."

Caitlin walked over to a long bundle wrapped in a heavy tarp and flipped it open. The tangle of pipes she had discovered in the service closet tumbled out and landed clanging on the deck. Caitlin nudged them with her boot. "These pipes were flooded with a spray of gamma rays. My guess is it happened when the crystal fracture occurred. It wouldn't have been obvious just by looking at them, but these pipes and tubes have all been contaminated, and so has the ... *product* that's been running through them." She flicked a look along the line of engineers. The expressions were all as stolid as before, except for one. Scott was frowning, his eyebrows pinching together in concern. He seemed about to move forward, and Caitlin quickly went on. "Fortunately, the contamination was low-level, within acceptable limits, and no permanent damage has been done. All known bottles of the hooch have been confiscated and destroyed by Dr. Boyce, and the same is going to happen to these pipes. The inspection scope hole will be repaired this afternoon. I don't intend to bring this matter up again, and I don't want any more engine-room hooch brewed up. Understand me, that is *no more hooch ever,* or there will be some serious penalties laid on the culprit. Is that clear?"

There was a soft chorus of "Yes, ma'am" and a nodding of heads all along the line. Scott swallowed and said, "Other ships have the tradition . . ."

"Other ships, Mr. Scott, are not the *Enterprise.* There are some traditions that should be put to rest. This is one of them, and stopping it starts now. Is *that* understood?" The acknowledging chorus came again. "All right, then. You're dismissed." They fell out, moving away quickly. Scott hesitated a moment and then hesitantly approached her.

"Commander Barry."

"Yes, Mr. Scott?"

"I'll have to take out a requisition form for a new tool kit. I think I've lost mine."

"No need. I found one in Service Closet 4. You must have misplaced it and forgotten about it."

"Oh, aye. That must've been it."

"It's still there. You can get it any time."

"Thank you, ma'am." He started to back away from her, but her voice stopped him.

"You'll find some pipe fittings and a couple of small jars have been removed from it. But they don't belong in a tool kit, anyway, do they?"

"No, ma'am."

"I didn't think so. Don't lose that kit again, Mr. Scott."

"No, ma'am. Never again." Scott turned and walked away.

The crew cabin was a single, smaller than Spock's but with enough room for one person to make himself at home. Even in the semidarkness, Spock was aware of the starkness of the decor. Either the occupant had not yet had time to add the homey touches that would make the cabin uniquely his own, or he preferred the plain standard-issue design. Spock guessed this particular crewman felt the severity of the unadorned cabin was more desirable. Everything of a personal nature was stowed in drawers and the closet. The room was kept warmer than most; Spock found it quite comfortable as he sat there waiting.

The surveillance equipment, tiny and unobtrusive, had been efficiently installed by engineering. Orloff alone had supervised the security arrangements Spock had specified, not without argument. Whatever transpired in this room would be transmitted audio-visually to several points on the ship where Pike and Number One, Orloff, and all the Vulcans on board would receive it. Spock felt it necessary that these be his witnesses.

The cabin door slid open, and a man stepped in. As the portal slid closed behind him, he reached out to touch a light sensor on the wall. A red-orange glow warmed the room, revealing Spock. The man jerked around toward him, startled.

"Lieutenant Spock. What're you doing here?"

Spock rose and moved a step forward. "Waiting for you."

"Is there something I can do for you?"

"I am here to discuss the murders of Commander Meadows and Lieutenant T'Pris and the theft of the Glory."

"I think the chief of security would be more helpful to you, Lieutenant."

Spock shook his head slowly, studying the man coldly. "He knows very little about Vulcans. This was a Vulcan crime from start to finish. Both Meadows and T'Pris were killed with the *lan-dovna* technique. The object of the crime was the Glory. Meadows was just a tool to acquiring it, but he had to die because he would reveal the criminal's identity. The first suspects were the Vulcans who had no alibi. We all thought only a Vulcan could possibly have committed the crime."

The other man stared at him, waiting, his face expressionless.

"Then the murderer made a mistake," Spock coldly went on. "He used the same method of execution on Lieutenant T'Pris when all the other Vulcans were under surveillance and I was on Areta. That was a stupid move, very non-Vulcan, because it exonerated all the *known* Vulcan crew. T'Pris may not have concluded the same thing I have—that the murderer must be a Vulcan who is not known to be one or is not obvious as one—but she was on the right trail to discover his identity.

"As soon as I considered all the implications, I realized how that could be, because I am half human and half Vulcan. My father's genes dominate, and I am physically more Vulcan than human. But go ahead a generation or two, breed a Vulcan-human to a human and then to a human again. Ultimately, the human side will dominate, in appearance and in all important physical aspects."

"It takes one to know one. Is that what you're saying?"

Spock ignored the comment. "T'Pris had been going back through the permanent records, the family histories of every crew member. I was able to reconstruct the trail of her investigation. You do not understand enough about the library computer to know that any record can be retrieved by a knowledgeable operator even if it has been erased. She was close to discovering what I did, that one man aboard who is seemingly human has a Vulcan heritage. It had to be you, Lieutenant Reed. You allowed Meadows to take the Glory from the vault, and your great-grandmother was the daughter of one of the high clans of Vulcan. I do not understand why the name in the records is given as T'Dess Alar-ken-dasmin. That is a matriarchal designation of house, a renunciation of her father's name."

"Why should she keep the name of a father who abandoned her after she was raped and nearly beaten to death by a human adventurer?" Reed snapped harshly. "She was an innocent, caught alone and savagely violated by an alien pig for his pleasure. He escaped Vulcan justice, but T'Dess's family couldn't bear the disgrace of what had been done to her. Her father cast her out, to live or die or make her way on her own. The only one who helped her was her mother. She gave T'Dess enough money to make passage to Earth. A fitting banishment, when you think of it."

Spock considered it, troubled by the story. "I can understand that. I do not understand how she was able to become pregnant with—"

"My grandmother." Reed grinned sardonically at Spock, enjoying himself for the moment. "You know, we heard about you, the great genetic accomplishment. The mating of a Vulcan and a human. You were famous on Vulcan. Created and produced by *almost* the finest geneticists in the known galaxy." He chuckled nastily. "A Vulcan conceit, Spock. Vulcan arrogance. Just because Vulcans hadn't tried it before, they thought it had never been done.

"But it had been. Privately funded genetics labs on Earth were way ahead of them on that kind of life engineering—had been for about a hundred years. The human T'Dess worked for as a servant was wealthy, and old, and had never had a child. T'Dess was grateful to him for taking her in. She agreed to marry him and bear the child the geneticists designed. Once my grandmother was born, they had the techniques down pat. After she married, Great-granddad wanted a grandchild to sit on his knee before he died. My father was created without half the trouble and in half the lab time as Grandmother. It's simple when you know how to do it, Spock. *You* were an idea whose time had come on Earth about sixty years before you were even thought of on Vulcan."

Spock's eyes strayed away from the man, considering the story. "Your family has a history of good citizenship on Earth. Why did you—" As he brought his head up, Reed drove at him, right hand stretched rigidly to deliver the *lan-dovna* hold to his throat. Spock lurched out of the way, off balance, but was caught by a glancing neck pinch that caused him to gray out for a moment. Reed shot past him as he tried to regain his senses. The door slid open and closed as the murderer fled into the corridor.

Spock cursed himself for seven kinds of a fool. He had forgotten his opponent was still part Vulcan, and the Vulcan traits of strength and quickness had apparently not faded, even though diluted by human blood. He ran for the door, knowing that Orloff would be activating security to try to head off Reed. He cursed himself again. The human—or was it Vulcan?—fault of vanity. He had been so sure he could confront and take the man by himself that he had insisted that Orloff not make many security precautions. The elevators would be covered, of course. As he glanced right and left, he saw Reed vanishing around a corner. There were no lifts in that direction, but there was a Jefferies tube.

Spock pulled his communicator, flipping open the lid. "Spock to security. Officer Reed is escaping Quarters Deck 4 utilizing the interconnecting service tube. I believe he will be heading for a transporter room. I am in pursuit." He bolted after Reed.

A Jefferies tube ran the length of the ship in several areas, connecting all decks and serving as a general maintenance corridor for a number of ship function networks. Shorter tubes in different areas had more specialized uses. The one Reed had ducked into was a major tube connecting with all deck levels. Reed had ignored the rungs of the ladder leading down the tube. Spock could see him far below, using the descent method of grabbing onto the sides of the ladder and sliding down, employing the feet as brakes. Even as Spock watched, Reed reached the level he wanted, stopped, and triggered the service door into the corridor. Spock did not waste time with the communicator. He jumped to the ladder and followed Reed down.

Security Lieutenant Bryce arrived at the door of Transporter Room 3 a step behind Spock. It was the only transporter room close to the exit of the Jefferies tube on this deck and the logical choice for Reed's escape. The door slid open at their approach, and they charged in to find the chief lying on the deck and the last vibrant humming of a beam-down fading away. Bryce quickly checked the downed chief while Spock examined the transporter controls. They would be locked on the coordinates Reed had chosen. Bryce looked up, nodding at Spock. "Only unconscious."

Spock slapped the intercom on the transporter console. "Spock to Pike."

"Here," Pike answered instantly.

"Reed has beamed down to the planet surface."

"Can you tell where?"

"The coordinates indicate the Druncara Range, sir."

"Mutant territory."

"I am beaming down after him, sir."

"Wait. I'd better come with you."

"Captain, there is no time to waste. I am beaming down alone . . . now."

"Spock, damn it—"

"Sir, it is my fault he escaped. I am taking the responsibility of bringing him back." He tapped off the intercom before Pike could reply and hurried toward the transporter platform, speaking over his shoulder to Bryce. "Activate the transporter as soon as I am on the pad, Lieutenant."

"Better take this with you." Bryce tossed Spock his own phaser pistol. He indicated the chief still unconscious on the deck. "He took the chief's phaser with him."

"Thank you, Bryce." Spock was positioned on the pad. "Energize."

Bryce carefully moved the energizing levers on the console. The deep-throated hum of the transporter began, quickly rising to a high whine as the spill of energy covered Spock's body, and he was gone.

Pike burst into the transporter room, saw the empty chamber, and whirled on Bryce. "You let him go."

"I don't think there was much I could have done to stop him, sir."

"Beam me down to those coordinates, Lieutenant."

"Yes, sir. If you order it, sir." Bryce slowly turned to the transporter console.

Pike hesitated, reconsidering it. Spock had wanted this to be his capture. He had said several times that it was a Vulcan matter, an affair of honor. Pike realized it was more than that to Spock. T'Pris's death weighed on Spock's mind. If Number One's theory was correct, the two were probably lovers. Pike knew that if he and Janeese had been on the same ship and she had been murdered, he would have allowed no one to stand in the way of his vengeance. A human emotion, an understandable one. And Spock was half human— fighting to hide it but subject to the demands it made on his emotions. Pike looked at Bryce and shrugged.

"Let's see how Spock handles it. Stay here until another transporter chief relieves you."

Boyce arrived at the transporter room with his medical bag and began to check the unconscious chief. He looked up at Pike and smiled. "Nothing more than a physical knockout, Chris. He'll be all right in a few more minutes." He bent over the man to administer further aid, and Pike moved to the intercom on the transporter console.

"Pike to Number One."

"Yes, sir."

"Can you track them on the planet surface?"

"We can detect the movement of life forms, sir. Unfortunately, the ones we perceive to be Lieutenant Spock and Lieutenant Reed are fairly close to others. We believe they may be mutants. If they commingle, we will not be able to tell one from the other."

"Stay on it, Number One. I'll be on the bridge in two minutes."

Chapter Thirteen

THE AREA SPOCK BEAMED INTO was rocky, lightly feathered with low-growing brush and a heavier line of trees. He immediately recognized it as the lower slopes of the Druncara Range. He could not place his position more exactly than that, but he was certain Reed could not know any more about the area, either. The desert was behind him; he judged Reed knew better than to go in that direction. Therefore, the only logical conclusion was that Reed had climbed up, deeper into the Range. He set off up the slope, his mind churning over the information he knew, trying to match it up to Reed's possible motives.

T'Dess Alar-ken-dasmin was listed in the Starfleet records as having been a house servant before her marriage. Simply put, she had begun her life on Earth as a menial. This was an intelligent woman who had been trained to manage a wealthy household, entertain for a socially prominent husband, and undoubtedly carry on a separate career of her own. Her knowledge, her bearing, and quite probably her beauty would have appealed to old Sanford Lynch. Marriage to Lynch would have given T'Dess back much of what she was born for, only not on her own planet. Not in the eyes of the high houses, especially her own. The *kahs-wan* taught Vulcans to survive when put to the test, and obviously T'Dess had done that. Spock could guess the bitterness that had lived in her. T'Dess would have had the training and the knowledge of history and tradition of all high-born Vulcan women, and she would have passed it down to her daughter, then to her grandson and great-grandson. But she also would have passed on the hate that she lived with.

Spock had just passed a tumble of boulders when a phaser set on kill blistered the air beside him. He instantly dived aside, rolled, and came up in the shelter of the rocks. "Reed!" he shouted.

"Give it up, Spock. I'll kill you, too."

"I cannot. If it is not me, it will be security beaming down. They will find you, even if you kill me. You have no hope of escaping." There was no reply to that, but Spock's sharp sense of hearing did not detect any sound of the man moving away. "Reed?"

"What?"

"Answers. I need to know."

"Curiosity killed the cat, Spock. Ever heard that one?"

"I am alive, Reed. I want answers. Why did you do it? For your great grandmother's honor? Yours? *Why?*"

There was a moment's pause, then Reed's voice drifted to him, quietly and almost dreamy, as though Reed were reflecting on it all. "She didn't hate Vulcan, you see, only the family that had abandoned her. In those days, Vulcan women were taught the same martial arts as men, not the way they're coddled now." He snorted derisively. "T'Pris was soft, and she died."

"You bastard," Spock hissed. He held himself from leaping toward Reed's hiding place only by great effort of will.

"As it happens, Spock, that's one charge I don't answer to. All my ancestors were legally married. I'm one-eighth Vulcan, completely Vulcan in my training and loyalty, but T'Dess's clan would never accept me as family."

"Your human blood never made you a criminal. What drove you to steal the Glory? To murder?"

There was a long silence, and then Reed's voice came down to him coldly, sardonically. "It's so simple, Spock. It's the Glory and my great-grandmother's house and their so-called honor."

Spock shook his head, nonplussed. "I do not understand the connection."

"You and your precious computers and all their information. Don't they have the information that my great-grandmother's patriarchal clan was the Archenida?" Spock's face changed with a sudden understanding, and it was almost as though Reed could see him. "Yes, the so-called protectors of the Glory."

"Again, I do not understand your reference. The so-called protectors?"

"You don't know, do you, Spock? No one does, and that's why I did it. The Archenida's proud clan heritage as the keepers and defenders of the Glory is a lie. T'Dess knew the secret, and each of her descendants has been told the truth about the Archenida and the Glory."

"We found them on Areta. The last keeper of the stone was of clan Archenida, laying down his life to protect it."

"Really? That's what they'd like to have all Vulcan believe. The fine and loyal protectors of the Glory were afraid to allow it to be exposed to the public. Someone might have designs on it. So they paraded a beautifully duplicated glass replica in all those ceremonials and show-the-flag missions. That was the stone that was lost, Spock. They still have the real gemstone on Vulcan, but they can never admit it. All their bravery in protecting the Glory, the loss they suffered when the ship and the Glory went missing— all that was bound up in a lie, Spock. A lie they could never reveal. *They* are the thieves of the Glory; they hold it still. But T'Dess knew the secret as a daughter of the house. She passed it on to her daughter and grandson and to me. She's still alive, you know."

Spock began inching his way around the huge tumble of boulders. If he could keep Reed talking, he might be able to distract him from the fact that Spock was circling around, trying to get behind him. "So when we found the Glory, you saw it as a golden opportunity for revenge."

"Meadows was easy. I told you that. He wanted to examine the Glory and was willing to lie to do it. I didn't know how I would get my hands on the stone before that, but he handed me the perfect opportunity. He took the Glory; he even signed for it. The security vault post is isolated, a dull duty, never checked by a superior officer. As soon as the corridors were clear, I followed Meadows to the lab where he was working on analyzing the stone. He already had the beginning tests in the library computer. He thought I was coming to reclaim the Glory, and I was, but not the way he thought. It was a simple thing to kill him. I took the Glory and erased the computer files he'd been working on. I put the stone in a safe place. You never found it, did you? T'Pris became a problem, though. She was onto the personnel files, and I couldn't let her find me out."

Spock had circled the boulders and homed in on Reed's voice. The man was hidden among the trees just beyond the boulders. Reed's last words infuriated Spock, but he drew himself back from the edge of an anger that could have driven him into a stupid move.

Slowly. He must move slowly.

Reed was still speaking as Spock eased himself forward into the area between the rocks and the trees. There was a small amount of low brush, and Spock crept forward carefully on his hands and knees into it.

"Do you understand it now, Spock? Does your Vulcan honor comprehend how much it means to me to bring T'Dess Alar-ken-dasmin back to Vulcan with our revenge? House Archenida must acknowledge what I've done to save their vaunted honor. They must acknowledge that I am T'Dess's great-grandson *and a true Vulcan*. It would be *ashv'cezh.*"

Spock had never felt the touch of the Vulcan concept of *ashv'cezh,* translated as "revenge worse than death." Reed's act, no matter how criminal, would expose the lies House Archenida had spun for centuries, and T'Dess would have her humiliation and abandonment avenged in the most psychologically vicious manner that could be imposed on Vulcans. It was brilliant.

Spock had made his way to a position at right angles to Reed. He couldn't speak, or he would give away where he was. His silence might provoke Reed, possibly cause the man to move out of cover where Spock could see him.

Suddenly, there was a rustle in the trees where Reed had taken cover. Reed called out in surprise and then fear. A movement behind him brought Spock around to face a group of mutants. One of them made to grab him and then pulled back at the sight of his Vulcan features. He put the phaser back on his belt and made a gesture of peace toward them as Panlow had taught them, and the mutants moved aside for him. Spock straightened up and stepped out of the brush. Looking toward the trees, he saw another group of mutants had disarmed Reed and were wrestling him into a cleared area. Spock moved forward, raising a hand toward the mutants, and called out in the Aretian tongue.

"Stop! If you are Panlow's people, you know me. Stay away from this man. He is a fugitive, and *he is mine!*"

The mutants paused, snapping looks between Reed and Spock. The one in the lead, a giant whose spine twisted into a hunched sideways position, waved a hand. "You have him." The mutants pushed Reed toward Spock.

Reed stared around wildly. "I'm an outcast, too. You know what that means. Help me. *Help me!*" His tone was clear, but his appeal in English fell on uncomprehending ears.

The mutants backed away, leaving Spock and Reed to face each other. Their meaning was also clear; it was not their quarrel. Whatever was between the normal and the mutant Spock was not their concern. Reed tried to lunge for the phaser one of the mutants held loosely in his hand, but Spock took a run and dived at him, bringing the security man crashing to the ground. Reed attempted to get a hand up to Spock's neck, but Spock twisted away and brought his knee up into Reed's gut. Not fancy, not even Vulcan, but it worked. Reed writhed in pain, allowing Spock to get to his feet. Reed still retained enough Vulcan strength to shake off the blow and stagger to his feet as Spock came at him again. Spock knew he was fighting without discipline, allowing rage over T'Pris's death to command him, but all he wanted was to punish Reed. He reached for Reed's neck with his right hand, intending to apply the *lan-dovna* hold. Reed batted his hand away, grabbed Spock's arm, and threw him.

Spock doubled his knees to his chest as Reed pounced on him and kicked the man away to the right. Reed scrambled in the dirt, and Spock fell on top of him again, reaching this time for a neck pinch. Reed wriggled away by twisting under him and with a great effort wound up atop Spock. The two had been evenly matched until now, but Reed was gasping, his strength starting to fail. Spock's hand shot for Reed's throat as the man heaved for air. The *lan-dovna* hold would cut off Reed's breath forever. Suddenly, Spock found his mind flashing on an image of T'Pris—gentle, patient, wise . . .

And unable to understand why her death would be celebrated with hate.

Spock's honor would be lost if he murdered Reed in cold blood. Spock's hand closed on the join of Reed's shoulder; and as he administered the neck pinch, Reed collapsed in a limp heap under him. Spock stayed there a moment, hovering over the body of his enemy, pulling his emotions in under a tight rein. Dimly, he became aware of an odd noise and looked up. The mutants were hopping up and down in some kind of celebration dance and grunting. From the twisted smiles on their faces, Spock came to the conclusion that they thought he had done the right thing. The mutant holding the phaser came forward and held it out to him, grinning in approval.

Spock took it, nodding his thanks. Then he reached for his communicator, flicked open the grid, and grated, "Spock to *Enterprise.*"

"Enterprise. *This is Pike.*"

"I have him, Captain. There will be two to beam up, as soon as I see some friends of ours out of the area."

"I beg your pardon?"

"I will explain later, sir."

Pike waited in the security office as Spock half hauled the still weak Reed before him. Reed pulled himself erect and managed a proud stance before Pike and Orloff.

"You've done well, Mr. Spock," Pike said. "I believe Commander Orloff can handle the security detail from here."

Reed spat on the deck and stared at them arrogantly. "I've beaten you all, anyway. When you find it—if you find it—you'll find the Glory is all I've said it was. A fake. A disgrace to the Archenida clan. And that's what I set out to do, to prove their honor and their legend is a lie."

"We *have* found it, Reed," Pike said flatly.

Reed and Spock both stared at Pike. Reed blurted out first. *"What?"*

"It was in the 'very safe place' you thought would be ideal to hide it. After Number One reported the complete sweep of the ship had found nothing, I wondered where someone on board might hide it so no one would think of looking there. I've read Poe, too, Reed. The obvious place to hide it is the place out in plain view—or, in this case, the one place no one would think to look. We found it in the security vault where you had replaced it in a different container."

Reed struggled with that a moment, his pride staggering under the apparent ease with which the captain had countered him. "Well, it doesn't matter that you found it. I've still shown up the conceit and the lies of the Archenida. I've shown that the heroic legend that surrounds them and the Glory was a prevarication from beginning to end."

Pike gestured to Orloff. "Commander, would you bring the stone here." The security chief moved forward with the huge emerald in his hands, and Spock looked down into the deep green stone that had caused so much havoc and death. "Spock, please call up the report on the analysis of the Glory that we had the geology lab run while you and Reed were on Areta."

Spock glanced sharply at Pike, then turned to the library-computer terminal on Orloff's desk. "Computer, show the analysis on Vulcan's Glory."

The screen on the gooseneck mount immediately began to flash up information. Spock scanned it as rapidly as it winked on the screen, and then he turned to Reed. "Audio analysis," he snapped. The library computer's female voice began to intone the carbon and mineral properties of the stone. Spock began to smile at Reed, not a pleasant smile at all. "You hear that, Reed? Do you understand the analysis? It *is* an emerald—not glass. The Glory is real. It was lost as the legend said. The only liar was T'Dess. She poisoned you all with her hate. If you had done nothing —if you had simply been a member of the *Enterprise* crew which had found and restored the Glory to Vulcan—you would have been a hero. You and she might have returned to Vulcan and been given the warm welcome you desired. But you listened to her lies, listened to her hate, and you have lost everything."

Reed's face buckled in anguish and frustration, but Spock wasn't looking at him. He was staring straight ahead and thinking, *And so have I. So have I.*

The *Enterprise* was en route from Areta to Vulcan. Pike had turned the bridge over to Number One and retired to his cabin, where he paced irritably while Phil Boyce reclined lazily in a form-molded chair and sipped at a snifter of Saurian brandy—the only liquor he currently trusted. "Two key scientists dead, one security guard in the brig charged with their murders, all in the space of ten days. I thought this would be just another mission."

"Those are the minuses," Boyce said easily. "Consider the pluses, Chris. The situation on Areta is even better than was originally projected. The fate of the *He-shii* and her crew was discovered. Vulcan's Glory was found and is being returned. Your new second officer proved to be reliable, resourceful, and talented. His intelligence goes without saying . . ."

"All right, agreed," Pike said. "But I can't help but think that we've lost something in Spock through all of this. I grant he doesn't have many reasons to smile right now, but he's colder, harder, more silent than before. More formal, if you can imagine."

"I noticed. Does it bother you, Chris?"

"I don't know." He corrected himself almost instantly. "Yes, it does. I liked the man I met two weeks ago. I'm not so sure about this change in him."

"Life changes us all, sometimes a lot more quickly than we'd like, but we don't often get to choose." Boyce sipped his brandy and then said calculatingly, "Then there's Number One."

Pike stopped pacing and swung around to stare at the doctor. "Number One? What has she got to do with this?"

"She's cool, often formal. You regard her as a good officer."

"Of course. The finest."

"You like her."

"Absolutely. The most professional first officer I've ever—"

"How about as a woman?"

"She's—" Pike shrugged. "Perfect."

"Most men say they're looking for a perfect woman."

"Phil, what are you up to?"

The doctor shrugged his shoulders innocently and took another sip of the brandy. "Nothing. Just pointing out some of the local attractions to someone who's been, mmm, scouting more exotic locales for quite some time now."

Pike studied the older man, frowning. Boyce looked up at him with a slight smile. "Leave before this last one, you came back raving about Janeese Carlisle. Holophotos, everything. You couldn't stop talking about her. I even heard about the ring you gave her. Not a real engagement, but the next thing to it. This time back, not a word. Gloom and depression. It doesn't take too much thought for an old veteran to figure out you and Janeese decided to call it quits."

"She did."

"It happens, Chris. And you changed some because of it, the same way Spock has changed since he lost T'Pris. Part of the lumps we take as human beings. T'Pris died—that's hard to accept for someone so young. What happened to you is a little more common. Someone we care deeply about just doesn't care as much about us. We feel we're less the man or woman we thought we were. That isn't so. Sometimes things just don't work out the way we want. Those are the chances we all take. I have. You have. And you know what, Chris? We'll keep on taking them. It's human nature."

Pike was silent for a moment, thinking it over. Then he looked up at Boyce. "You were talking about Number One."

"Was I? Well, she's an interesting woman."

"Yes," Pike said thoughtfully.

"And she's perfect."

The entire senior command of the *Enterprise* paid their respects to T'Pris's family at the estate where her body had been borne to lie in state. Pike, Number One, Boyce, Caitlin Barry, and the other officers, all in dress uniforms, passed quietly before Sirak and T'Dar to murmur condolences for the loss of their daughter. Spock stood apart, as a representative of his father's house, not as an *Enterprise* officer. The other Vulcan crew members were ranked behind him, respectful delegates of their own houses, paying homage to a colleague.

The ship's officers were greeted and thanked by T'Pris's family and then led to the large circle among the trees that formed the estate's shrine. The ancestral figures that decorated it traced the clan's history to its beginnings. The geometric sculptures in the center of the sand-floored shrine were carved from native Vulcan jade that glowed a rich teal blue in the lowering sun. A catafalque rested before them.

The ceremonial drum beat slowly, accompanied only by the lonely sound of a Vulcan flute to lead in the six men who carried T'Pris's casket. They solemnly lowered it to rest on the catafalque. The other

Vulcans followed it in and arranged themselves around the edges of the shrine's circle. Sirak strode to the central platform and bowed to the four cardinal directions. Then he faced the casket and bowed to it.

"T'Pris, beloved child, you gave us great joy in your living. You graced us with your beauty, with your spirit, with your love. Your time with us was not long, and we have no more of you than what is here." He gestured sorrowfully toward the casket. "Yet we celebrate the memories of you that will stay in our hearts, alive and vibrant as you always were. As long as each of us lives, so long shall you remain alive. And to each succeeding generation, as each of us knew T'Pris, we vow to pass on our memory of her, so there is no dying but only a renewal of love each time her name is spoken and her story is told."

Sirak again bowed to the casket and then to the four directions. Quietly, then, he led the way out of the circle, each person moving past the casket and laying a hand on it briefly in passing. The ceremonial drummer pounded out the slow thrumming beat of the dirge interwoven with the poignant sound of the flute as they passed by.

Spock was the last to move. As he reached out to touch the deep black polished wood of the casket, he shuddered and had to pause, head down, to control the deep sorrow that shook him. "T'Pris," he whispered softly. "T'Pris, I vow I will never forget." *I gave myself to you freely,* he thought. *We chose each other. There will never be another like you in my heart.*

"Lieutenant Spock," Sirak said quietly as he moved to his side. "Are you indisposed?"

"No," Spock said, straightening. "I am only moved by the loss of a colleague . . . and a friend. The greater loss is yours. My family sends its deepest regrets."

"We are honored," Sirak replied formally, "that the son of Sarek of the House of Surak found merit in our daughter."

"More than merit, sir," Spock said. "T'Pris was . . . an exceptional woman. Exceptional." He nodded to Sirak and held up his hand in the Vulcan salute. "Live long and prosper."

Sirak gave the traditional reply. "Peace and long life."

Spock nodded, but he felt there would be no peace for him, and that even if he did have a long life, it would be made lonely by the lack of T'Pris's love in it.

He turned away and followed his fellow officers, who were some distance ahead of him. He went slowly, the salute ringing in his ears.

Number One sat in the command chair, musing over the ceremony that signified T'Pris's departure from life. It had been gentle and dignified, as T'Pris had been. Number One thought she would not mind a Vulcan ceremony to commemorate her own memory when her turn came.

She glanced over at Spock, quietly working at the library computer. Since T'Pris's death, he had become more silent and conversely more abrupt when he did speak. Vulcans supposedly had no emotions. She wondered whether that wasn't as big a subterfuge as Reed's great-grandmother had spun, a lie taken on for protection. She'd probably never know, but she did know Spock was hurting. Her ruminations were interrupted by Pike's brisk arrival from the lift. She automatically vacated the command chair and moved to her station at the helm as he stepped down into the well of the bridge.

"Number One, take us out of orbit and set a course for Starbase 12. I've just received a message from Starfleet that the ambassadorial party from Delta Indus II was dropped off there by a passenger vessel that developed warp problems. We've been ordered to transport them on to their home planet."

"Aye, sir," Number One snapped as she worked her fingers lightly over her console. "Breaking out of standard orbit."

Beside her, Lieutenant Andela tapped coordinates into the navigation console and intoned, "Laying in a course for Starbase 12."

"Warp factor four."

"Aye, sir."

"Oh, and Number One . . ."

"Sir?" She turned to look at him questioningly, her long black hair swinging forward to catch on her shoulder and frame her face.

"See me for dinner tonight. Nineteen hundred in my quarters all right with you?"

She stared at him blankly. "Dinner?"

"Ah, yes. Business," Pike said. "We have to discuss the ship's operations. You'll have the mission log up to date by then, won't you?"

"It's up to date now, sir."

"Of course. Well, we'll discuss it."

"Aye, sir. Dinner. Nineteen hundred. Your quarters."

She turned back to her console, puzzled. *He's never*

done that before. On the other hand, the first time for anything was always interesting. She ran her eyes over her board and then up at the viewscreen, where the fathomless black of space sparkled with faraway stars. "We are out of orbit, on course for Starbase 12. Warp factor four."

She hit the warp control, and the *Enterprise* leaped forward—toward the stars and a new mission.

Afterword

In 1986, Dave Stern, then editor for Pocket Books' *Star Trek* line, approached me about the possibility of writing an original novel for the series. I immediately said, "Yes"—and immediately wondered what story I should pitch. Any number of possibilities existed in the ongoing world of "Classic Trek" novels where Kirk, Spock, McCoy, and company battled the Klingons, the Gorns, and others, and boldly . . . well, you know.

On the other hand, I did have one distinct advantage going for me. I was there in 1963 when Gene Roddenberry created the whole thing. In 1964, I was the one who typed up the clean copy of Gene's script for "The Cage," the initial pilot for the series. I was there in 1966 when the decision was made to combine that episode with additional material (dubbed "the envelope") to create the two-part story titled "The Menagerie." To avoid just throwing away what had been a very expensive pilot film, it was necessary to incorporate James T. Kirk, Dr. McCoy, and other new characters into the earlier world of Captain Christopher Pike. The two-parter established a close connection, via Mr. Spock, between the voyages of the *U.S.S. Enterprise* under the command of different captains. I knew how Gene originally envisioned Pike, how his character might have developed, and his relationship with Spock.

The more I thought about it, the more a story involving young Lieutenant Spock and Chris Pike intrigued me. It also gave me an opportunity to delve into Scotty's initial voyage on the *Enterprise*—a lieutenant (j.g.) with an untamed sense of mischief and a remarkable skill at making engine-room hooch. Well, after all, not only was he a Scott, he was a *Scot*.

Then there was Vulcan. Theodore Sturgeon introduced a number of cultural and historical precedents in his script "Amok Time." In terms of production, it was done on one stage with a relatively small cast of actors portraying Vulcans—truly a magnificent feat of costume, makeup, and set design conveying the sense of an entire world and its society.

I keyed on Ted's base in writing "This Side of Paradise" and "Journey to Babel." The characters referenced it, but I didn't have to depict Vulcan itself. Without meaning to, I became the de facto expert on Spock, his family, and his planet. Even after *Trek* went off the air and the next opportunity came along in animation, the Vulcan thing was in my mind.

Animation offered new vistas for us as storytellers. We didn't have to worry about zippers showing or extraterrestrials always being humanoid. Alien environments were a snap—just draw them. As a result, I could call for some of Vulcan's vast arid desert and the capital city of ShiKahr in the script of "Yesteryear," and even show a massive *sehlat* character, which could only be talked about on the original series.

As for depicting all that in a novel—no problem. The real complication wasn't in the description of the world. Who were the people? What was the history? Could I have some fun and tell a story the fans would enjoy? The more

I thought about it, the more Spock's first assignment to the *Enterprise* intrigued me. The audience had seen Christopher Pike only in a two-part episode. More important, the vigorous man who captained the ship was depicted in only half of that story. The rest of the time, he was a crippled wreck worthy of our admiration, but also drawing forth our pity. What was he like *before* that story, which was the only one the audience knew? I had to figure it out, because the voyage I had in mind was *only* in my mind. No one else onscreen or in a novel had taken that journey, and I had to break new ground to do it.

First, I could conjure a Vulcan completely free of anyone else's influences or ideas. I didn't have to worry about how it would be seen. Prose allows the creation of its own landscapes. I could delve deep into the complicated Spock–Sarek–Amanda relationships for the depth of feeling that underlay them. Yes—feeling. Everyone knew Vulcans were emotional; they just controlled and hid their emotions better than anyone else in the galaxy. Well, our galaxy anyway. Spock could be shown at this critical moment in his life, caught between the demands and expectations of his father and the needs and ideas he experienced as his own person. He had to deal with an arranged marriage, one about which he had enormous doubts, one that would later lead to the events of "Amok Time."

One of the things I liked about writing "Vulcan's Glory" was the fact that I could explore the character of Number One, the *Enterprise*'s previous, mysterious, executive officer. I sat down for a couple of hours with Majel Barrett to discuss what she thought of the female officer she depicted in "The Cage." She gave me her ideas about what Number One felt and thought, and the fact that on Ilyria, her planet of origin, she would have been the best of her breed for the year she was born, the most genetically perfect being. Majel also thought Number One had an emotional thing for Pike—and he would be inclined to reciprocate, except for the restraining fact that he was her commanding officer.

I also had the opportunity to give the chief engineering position to a woman, something I tried to do a little later on *Star Trek: The Next Generation*, only to have the character bumped in favor of a male Irish engineer. No disrespect to Colm Meany, an excellent actor, but do engineers *have* to come only in masculine British models? Just for fun, I gave my chief engineer the name of a friend's young daughter, Caitlin Barry. For years, little Caitlin brought out the book to show her friends and point out that she was an important character. *And* an engineer.

Most of all, I could create the history of "The Glory," the great jewel prize that was lost centuries ago and found again on this voyage. This artifact harked back to the time when Vulcans were still savage and emotional and fought wars among themselves. I consulted with a gemologist to get the parameters of an unusually large, uncut, and nearly flawless emerald (one of my favorite gemstones) and gave it a back story that I hoped would intrigue the readers.

Oh, yes—one other little detail. Filling out four hundred pages of typed manuscript required a bit more story than just locating and retrieving a highly valuable artifact. There were two love stories and a mystery and an action adventure tale as well.

I hope you've enjoyed them and found the characters of Spock, Scott, Pike, Number One, and Caitlin Barry intriguing and likable companions on this voyage of the *Enterprise*.

D. C. Fontana
October 2005